George Lambert

The Power of Gold

Vol. I

George Lambert

The Power of Gold
Vol. I

ISBN/EAN: 9783337047788

Printed in Europe, USA, Canada, Australia, Japan

Cover: Foto ©Andreas Hilbeck / pixelio.de

More available books at **www.hansebooks.com**

VOL. I.

THE POWER OF GOLD

A NOVEL

BY

GEORGE LAMBERT

For 'tis a question left us yet to prove
Whether Love lead Fortune, or else Fortune Love.
Hamlet.

IN TWO VOLUMES.

VOL. I.

LONDON:
HURST AND BLACKETT, PUBLISHERS,
13, GREAT MARLBOROUGH STREET.
1886.

THE POWER OF GOLD.

CHAPTER I.

FATHER, SON, AND DAUGHTER.

IT is by no means an easy matter to find
out what a man is by his 'outer present-
ment;' of course there are certain plainly-
defined differences, and, though the sumptuary laws have long ago gone to limbo,
and the Sunday suit of the artisan is not
so very far removed from the Sabbath
attire of what the catechism calls his
'betters;' though the 'servant-gal' emerges
on her 'Sunday-out' from the chrysalis
form of every-day attire, and takes the
arm of her 'young man' at the top of the

area-steps in raiment which is a fair copy
of 'missus's;' yet, at the same time, it
would be difficult to mistake a navvy for
a city clerk, or a factory-lass for a 'young
lady' in a shop.   Things have, however,
become considerably mixed in the matter
of clothes, and the unoccupied wayfarer,
as he pursues his aimless course, can, if he
be of a speculative turn of mind, find
plenty of scope for his imagination in wondering what may be the occupations and
social status of the various passers-by.

More often than not he will be mistaken.
That elegantly-attired individual, strolling
gently down Piccadilly with a cigar in his
mouth, well-gloved and booted, and with
the neatest of umbrellas, *looks* like what
the cabmen call 'a swell;' but put some
question to him, as to your best way to
such-and-such a street, for instance—and
the words of his mouth, decided in their
London twang, and wanting in the fatal
aspirate, will disclose him as a cockney of

the purest type; a gentleman of the great
order of the commercial perhaps, just off a
journey, and refreshing himself, after that
strenuous pushing for 'orders' which
competition has brought about, with a
look at the 'nobs;' with a sincere feeling
of satisfaction in his mind that his 'get-
up' is irreproachable, and not unlikely to
cause folk to make the very mistake you
have made.

There are, on the other hand, noblemen
of very high degree indeed, who might
easily be taken for pork-butchers, and who,
were they endued with the white apron of
that fraternity, would look quite in their
place behind a counter, with a chopper in
their hands, a large dish of sausages in
front of them, and chines, and legs, and
shoulders of pig hanging around in graceful festoons.

Now Squire **Armer**, of Coombridge
Manor, near Exeter, was the **very 'moral'**
of a country squire. Look at him as he sits

at breakfast this summer morning with
Nellie, his daughter, and Jack, his son and
heir. If ever a man looked his part, surely
Squire Armer looks his. Of middle height,
sixty years old, stoutly built, ruddy-
cheeked, blue-eyed, clean-shaven, save for
about an inch of greyish whiskers, the
bald patch on the top of his head framed
round with short-clipped, curly grey hair,
clad in a many-pocketed shooting-coat,
with his shapely lower limbs encased in
breeches and gaiters, Mr. Armer looks
exactly like Punch's pictures of John Bull,
and savours strongly of the home-farm,
the covert side, tramps through stubble
and turnips after 'birds,' the magisterial
bench, and all the other occupations of
the county magnate. And yet Squire
Armer had passed the greater part of his
existence in the city of London : he knew
intimately all the ins-and-outs of that
noisy habitation of Mammon, and was, not
so very long ago, particularly well acquaint-

ed with the staid frock-coat, the conventional pepper-and-salt continuations, and the abominable stove-pipe head-gear of the orthodox city man. His portly figure had been well-known on the Stock Exchange, and his signature was still 'good' for very respectable sums of money in the many lanes and alleys of the money-grubbing Babylon.

John Armer had been, in fact, a stock-broker, and his name still appeared in the well-known firm of Armer and Gidley. Indeed, the bulk of his property was still in the firm, and the squire now and again sought the dingy precincts of the office, though he left Mr. Gidley, his partner, to do almost what he liked with his capital. Now Mr. Gidley was a born worshipper at the shrine of Mammon, and Armer's love of the country, which prompted many long absences from the city, and at length ended in the purchase of Coombridge Manor, and his virtual retirement from the cares of business, seemed a species of madness to his partner, who thought the air of London the finest in the world, who could find virtues even in black and yellow fogs, and who desired no better lot than to pass his life between his office in the city, and his home in Bedford Square.

There is not much of the 'city man,' however, in Squire Armer now, as he stows away a plentiful breakfast, chatting pleasantly with his daughter the while. A pretty picture is that breakfast-room with its well-spread table, and the bright summer sun glinting on the silver urn, making the china seem almost transparent, and bringing out all the beauties of the flowers with which the white-covered table is plentifully adorned.

'Jack,' said the squire to his son, as he finished his 'second cup.' 'Just hand me over the *Times*, my boy.'

'In one minute, father,' said Jack, 'I'm just looking to see whether . . . . Well!'

he exclaimed, at that instant catching sight of something in the voluminous columns. 'Well! I'm . . . blest!' (with a suspicious pause before the 'blest,' as if he gulped down some rather stronger expletive). 'I'm blest if I haven't passed, after all! Behold in me a bloated Bachelor of Arts!'

'No, Jack!' said his sister Nellie, running over to him and looking over his shoulder; 'do let me see it, where is it? So it is. I *am* so glad,' she added, as Jack pointed to the column where under the heading of 'University Intelligence' was printed, at the tail end of the third class in history, the words, 'Armer J. Trin :'

'Jack, my son,' said the squire, rising and shaking hands with Jack after the manner of Britons in such cases of sudden emotion, 'this is the best piece of news I've heard for a long time, and I frankly confess it is all the more welcome because unexpected.'

' Well,' said the ingenuous Jack, ' I freely own it *is* a trifle unexpected by me, too, though old Blower' (so he designated that well-known ' coach,' the Reverend H. Blower) ' *did* say he thought I *might* get through by the skin of my teeth.'

' How funny it looks to see you in print, Jack,' said his sister, gazing at the all-important syllables in the paper. ' There will be no bearing with you now, Mr. Bachelor, though I am sure you are conceited enough already; it would have done you good to have been " plucked," or " ploughed,"—which is it ?—again, though you must be used to the process by this time.'

' Helen Armer,' returned Jack, with much solemnity, ' I would have you remember to whom you are speaking in that flippant manner ; but a Bachelor of Arts can afford to despise the unsophisticated utterances of a young girl. It all comes of the higher education of women ;

oh! for those blessed days when one's sisters devoted their time and energies to the still-room . . . .'

'Father,' exclaimed Nellie, laughing, and interrupting Master Jack's elegant periods, 'just listen to Jack; what magnificent language! you know, Jack, it is all nonsense, and, if it had not been for me, you never would have passed at all.'

'You *were* good, I must own, Nellie,' said Jack, 'and you certainly had a stiffish job to make your lazy brother work; so you shall come up to Cambridge, and see the gorgeous fruits of your labours; you shall see me "take my degree;" an awesome process, I can tell you. Eh! father, you will bring Nellie up, won't you?'

'Young man,' said his father, 'this degree of yours has cost me something very like two thousand pounds, you extravagant young dog, and I shall most certainly see what I have got for my money, and Nellie

shall come too.   Now,' continued the squire,
rising from his chair, and throwing down
the *Times,* ' I am going down to the farm ;
come you too, Jack.'

Jack followed his father into the hall,
whence the squire called out to his daughter, ' Nellie, what are you going to do to-
day ?'

'Oh ! I've heaps of letters to write, and
I am going to "do" the flowers, and see the
cook, and all sorts of things, and . . . .
Jack !' she called out to her brother, ' mind
you don't let father be late for lunch, for
you and I are going to the Dentons this
afternoon you know.'

' All right !' said Jack, as he closed the
hall door and hastened after his father.

Lazy, indeed, Master Jack was, and lucky
was it for that young man that he was
' born with a silver spoon in his mouth,'
for he certainly was not of the stuff successful men are made of.   Good-natured,
somewhat selfish withal, and with quite a

sufficiency of conceit, with good looks and
ordinary abilities, young Jack Armer belonged to that large contingent who are
said sometimes to be ' nobody's enemy but
their own,' but who not unfrequently cause
a considerable amount of pain, not to say
anguish, to their very nearest and dearest.

To work, we are told, is natural to man ;
indeed, it is a remark occasionally heard
from the pulpit ; and though a proper senti-
ment of decency, not to speak of the prospect
of being taken up for ' brawling,' with a
penalty of not more than five pounds to
follow, prevents the hearer from interrupting the preacher, yet his thoughts are
his own, and he wonders whether that
learned gentleman has ever met with a
labouring man who has just dropped into a
legacy. Does the horny-handed one work
in such a case ? Alas ! for the *naturalness* of
work, not one heave of pick or delve of
spade, too probably, does he condescend to
until all the money has been melted into

liquid, and poured down his own and his
friends' gullets, if, indeed, Death does not
overtake him in his cups, and seize upon him
as another victim to repeated 'overdoses of
alcohol.' Or did the first discoverer of the
Pacific Islands find the nature's children,
who inhabited those balmy regions, work-
ing? I trow not! So long as their kind
mother Earth supplied them with all the
necessities, and even the comforts, of life
gratis, they were quite willing to abide by
this one-sided bargain, and only varied the
monotony of their diet by occasionally
devouring ' the stranger within their gates,'
or some vanquished enemy. Not until the
blessings of civilisation made them acquainted with rum as a decided improvement
upon 'kava,' (their nasty national drink)
and aprons, and petticoats, and poke
bonnets, and top hats as fashionable articles
of attire, did they dig and delve, and plant
and sow, to get obfuscated with the rum,
and to find the wherewithal to purchase

the often hideous clothes of the Western world, in the place of their own pretty coverings of flowers and fringes.

Now young Jack Armer was another instance of the *non*-naturalness of work. His father was undoubtedly a wealthy man, and nobody was in the least surprised that his son, with such excellent prospects, and not a particle of ambition, should be inclined to only one kind of work, namely, the arduous occupation of amusing himself. It is true he was perfectly willing to exert himself even strenuously, in *this* direction, and to devote large slices of time and a vast expenditure of muscular power in the pursuit of pleasure : whether through his father's preserves with a friend or two, dogs, a gun and a keeper, or in following the various packs of hounds within get-at-able distance from Coombridge, or in dancing far on into the small hours of the night; but of work, properly so called, the young man knew nothing, unless the hasty cramming into his brain (by means of 'cribs' and 'memoria technica,' invented by an ingenious 'coach') of a sufficiency of facts to satisfy the not too-exacting examiners, can be called by such a name.

Jack had made his sister Nellie the confidante of such of his escapades as could be narrated to her willing ears, and Nellie, a shrewd and sensible little woman, knew enough of her volatile and easy-going brother to make her feel anxious about his future. Many times, as she was well aware, had the squire put his hands into his pockets to pay son Jack's bills, though son Jack already had a more than sufficient allowance; and she also knew (a fact hidden, as yet, from the squire) that her incorrigible brother was again in his normal condition of insolvency, and that more requisitions on 'the governor' were impending.

Squire Armer could, on occasion, exhibit a very violent temper; he possessed also a large fund of obstinacy; unhappy 'scenes' between father and son had been not unfrequent of late, and Nellie dreaded the revelations which must perforce be made now that Jack was to take his degree and 'go down' for good. Still he *had* passed, and the squire, in his delight at this opportune success, might be inclined to be merciful, and once more to 'pay up,' and forget and forgive, and to afford the sinner another of those 'fresh starts with a clean slate,' which had hitherto only ended in new embarrassments and larger scores than ever on the said slate.

Nellie, then, had enough to think of—to say nothing of certain *personal* hopes and fears which were beginning to exercise her mind just then—as she stood for a few moments leaning against the windowframe, looking after her father and her brother as they walked on together, until they reached the corner of the drive and passed out of sight.

A tiny little maid was Helen Armer, fair-haired, blue-eyed, of a perfect little figure, with a delicate complexion, regular features, and the prettiest smile in the world. Small as she was, and fragile as she looked, she was a strong and healthy girl, and just as able to do a day's work in the saddle, or on the tramp, as many of her bigger and more robust-looking compeers. Good-natured, unselfish, and loving, there was yet a dash of sharpness in her character, and a certain spice of originalty, which, together with her quaint little china-shepherdess style of beauty, made her remarkable even among the beautiful women of favoured Devonia. Her mother had died when Nellie was still a child, and since she was twelve years old the squire, who never would let his little daughter be out of his sight for long, had made a companion and friend of her.

Thus she was more formed in her character at her present age of eighteen than most girls are at that age, in spite of the high-pressure system of education to which the nineteenth century young woman is subjected.

Confidence in the almighty self this system may produce, it may also result in a certain contempt for the experience and opinions of elders, not to speak of a slightly vulgar (shall we say?) propensity to 'shine' and astonish; which propensity is wont to develop, in some cases, into fastness, and a devotion to the 'chic,' and, in others, into the wearisome twaddle of the 'advanced' blue-stocking.

Neither 'blue' nor 'fast' was Nellie, but just an honest, healthy-toned English girl, exceedingly pretty, and clever, and witty withal; no wonder, then, that Squire Armer was proud and fond of his daughter, and that the undecided character of brother Jack found in his little sister's

sturdy common-sense and ready wit a welcome help in his many scrapes and follies.

Coombridge Manor-house nestled cosily
in a sort of dent in the side of a high hill;
behind the house the hill rose, clad to its
very summit with a plantation of firs, the
dark Scotch contrasting with the lighter
green of the feathery larch. A fair vision
met Nellie's gaze as she paused for a few
moments, looking out over the valley,
before she turned to her various domestic
avocations. The house was so placed that
from the front a green valley opened out
into a vast and varied view, whose furthest
limit was the glint of the distant sea.
Hill and dale, here a white village cluster-
ing round its ancient church tower, there a
golden patch of yellow gorse, fields of the
green springing corn, steep pitches clothed
with plantations, the bright sunlight over
all, and the soft clouds casting now and
again their flitting shadows; it was enough
to move even the most prosaic of men,

and to incline him to 'drop into poetry' à
la Silas Wegg.

A clump of huge trees before the house
gave a pleasant sound of rustling leaves,
and the faint murmur of a little brook in
the valley below, as it fretted on its course
over the rocks and stones which formed
its uneasy bed, came softly and soothingly
to the ear.   When Mr. Armer bought the
place, the Manor-house was in a most ruin-
ous state; built of the granite of the
country, it stretched a wide frontage to
the valley; its mullioned windows yawned,
empty of glass, and the ivy covered the
house even to the roof.   Very picturesque
was the old mansion in its decay, and
charming to the eye; but painful was the
havoc old Time had played with the
interior, and the would-be purchaser felt
some qualms as to the serious question of
cost, as he went from room to room, and
floor to floor.

The place had been in the market for

some time, for the family to whom the property belonged were too poor to live there, mortgaged as it was, and the then owner, the moment he came into the place, determined to sell it as soon as he could, and have done with what was, for a poor man, a hopeless job. As soon as the legal preliminaries were over which placed Mr. Armer in the proud position of owner of Coombridge, lord of the manor thereof, and possessor of a comfortable number of acres in that exceedingly hilly parish, the new squire had set to work with a will, and in a few months, in spite of the maddening slowness of the Devonshire labourer and artisan, the house was finished, fitted, and furnished, and ready for its occupants. Mr. Armer had carefully insisted that all that could be preserved of the old Manor-house should be kept exactly as it was, and that all new work should be done on the lines of the old; so the fine ancient front looked down the valley as of old, while the interior of the mansion was a monument to Mr. Armer's good taste, and very comfortable withal.

CHAPTER II.

THE DENTONS' 'AL FRESKY.'

LUNCH was over at Coombridge, and Mr.
Armer, Nellie, and Jack were chatting in
the porch, waiting for the dog-cart to come
round. The grinding of the wheels was
soon heard, and Tucker, the neatest and
deftest of young grooms, drew up exactly
at the right spot, jumped down, and stood
at the horse's head.

'You will have a splendid drive, Nellie,'
said Mr. Armer, as he helped his daughter
to the high seat beside her brother.

'I wish *you* were coming, father,' replied
Nellie; 'though,' she bent down and whis-
pered, 'you *do* abominate the unfortunate
Dentons.'

The squire shook his head, making a grimace savouring slightly of disgust.

'Take care of Nellie, Jack,' said he; and, after watching them till they were out of sight, he turned into the house.

When Mr. Armer bought Coombridge, there was no approach to the place from the main road but up a steep and rutty lane, and one of the first things the squire did was to make a long drive down the valley which the house fronted. It was down this drive that Jack was coaching his sister, on the way to Wreford, the Dentons' place. Through an avenue of beech-trees the road passed, till the brook was reached, when the drive struck off to the left, and followed the course of the little stream for nearly a mile, till the lodge was reached, and the gate which gave access to the road. And a lovely approach it was, tree-shaded, with the brook and its fern-covered banks on the right, and on the left the steep side of a wood-covered hill, at this season carpeted with flowers. The horse was fresh, and Jack's time was fully taken up in attending to his coaching for the first quarter of a mile, when Trumpeter settled down into something like steadiness, and made conversation on Jack's part possible.

'Comfortable, Nellie?' he asked.

'Yes, Jack,' she answered. 'This is a splendid dog-cart; it does not shake one's bones at all. I think this kind of carriage is quite the best for Devonshire; you can see over the high hedges sometimes.'

Jack and Nellie chatted away on general topics until the groom jumped down to open the gate, and walk up the long hill up which their road led.

'What a nuisance it is to have to take Tucker!' said Nellie. 'I have to think of everything I say; and, Jack, I *wish* you would be more careful, for every word you utter is repeated in the kitchen, and becomes the common property of Coombridge parish; sometimes I positively shudder at the free remarks you indulge in about our neighbours.'

'All right, Nellie,' said Jack. 'I'm sure I've been a perfect angel to-day, anyhow, for you have not told me yet about these Dentons; I forgot to ask you before, and, though positively burning for information, I nobly restrained myself. Why does father hate them so?'

'Well,' replied Nellie, 'it is their gorgeousness, I believe; you know father hates all display, and the Dentons' magnificence is something appalling. When we called a week or two ago, a solemn gentleman in black opened the door, a troop of bepowdered and silk-stockinged individuals stood about the hall, and, in fact, the whole scene struck me as being something stagey; the furniture is all gold and glitter, and the Dentons are gold and glitter personified.'

'What sort of a man is old Denton?' asked Jack.

'Mr. Denton père,' answered Nellie, 'is quite the best of them all; he is about sixty, I should think, bluff and what you call "jolly" in his manners; short, stout, and round-faced. He looks quite odd and out of place in all the splendour of Wreford, and, I fancy, the gentleman in black and the canary-coloured footmen rather patronise him.'

'I say, Nellie,' said Jack, 'you ought to write a novel; your descriptions are lovely.'

'Oh, everybody writes novels now-a-days,' said Nellie. 'It is quite distingué *not* to have written one.'

'Of all the conceit!' exclaimed Jack. 'Now let us have the girls.'

'There are two girls,' said Nellie, 'and there is nothing *real* about either of them. The eldest, who rejoices in the name of Theresa, is very handsome indeed. She is large, and she gushes. "So *very* kind of you to call! Isn't it a *lovely* day? Don't you *adore* Devonshire? We hear

Coombridge is quite *too* perfect,"' mimicked the wicked Nellie. 'The other one,' she went on, 'affects the languid, invalid style of manner; she drawls in a way that irritates me even to torture. "Don't you find the air of this county vewy twying, Miss Armer?" she droned out to me. "One always feels so tired, don't you know." I have no patience with her; she looks, and I am sure *is*, quite as strong as you or I, and I really felt as if I should have *liked* to have given her a good shaking.'

'And Mrs. Denton?' queried Jack, much amused.

'She was out when we called, and *I* was out when they returned the call, and you know they were engaged when we asked them to lunch, so I have never seen *her*. But oh! Jack, my *dear* Jack . . . the young man! he is *too* awful. Long, thin, stooping, with a sickly pale face and fish-like eyes, his hands dangling and his knees

knocking together, he is a perfect carica-
ture of the worst type of the exploded
æsthete. How on earth he came to be
the son of his round and tubby little father
is one of those things that "no fellow can
understand." He lithpth, Jack! it's *too*
lovely. He said to me, "Ithn't there
thomething tholemn in the thound of the
ruthtling of the leavth among the treeth."
That was the first thing he said to me,
and I had to bite my lips, or I should have
laughed, which would have been dreadful.
They say he has a room upstairs all blue
china, and old oak, and that kind of thing,
and that he is writing a poem. Imagine
the poem, please! But *I* believe he is a
lazy, weakly kind of man, and sits in his
æsthetic den like the country-folk here in
church on Sundays, "thinkin' o' nothin'."
He will be quite a nice friend for you,
Jack,' concluded Nellie, with a malicious
little smile. 'You say there is no one
here for you to "chum" with; behold

your opportunity in 'Enery Denton, as his father calls him.'

'After your graphic description, I don't think he is the kind of man I care about,' said Jack. 'There used to be some men like that up at Trinity; wore their hair about their ears, dressed in velvet with turn-down collars, loafed about in one another's rooms all day, and called boats and cricket and football "coarse." They looked as if they did not do much in the tub line. Everybody laughed at them, and I believe it is dying out now; but *they* didn't care, bless you, they thought themselves martyrs, and called us Goths, or Vandals, or Philistines, or something or other. A set of asses!' added Mr. Armer, junior, with supreme contempt.

Here they reached the top of the long hill, and the groom jumped up behind, putting an end to all conversation save that of the most ordinary nature.

It was not long before they reached the

resplendent blue and gold painted gates which formed the magnificent entrance to the Wreford domain, and gave good promise of the splendours to come. Two or three carriages were seen winding up the slight but long ascent which led to the house.

'A big meet,' said Jack; ' that explains the unwonted gorgeousness of your attire, eh, Nellie ?'

' What do you mean by " gorgeousness," Jack ?' asked Nellie. 'I purposely dressed as quietly as I could, for I think little people should not be too accentuated.'

' Oh, heavens !' exclaimed Jack. ' Accentuated ! what a word ! do you think *I* am accentuated enough for this kind of thing ? By all that's beautiful !' he added, ' there's a fellow with a top hat on just getting out of that wagonette, shiny shoes, and a frock coat ! by George !' and Jack regarded his suit of ' dittos ' and his not too elegant shoes with extreme disfavour.

Just then he had to concentrate his attention upon driving up to the hall door of
Wreford with that elegance and finish
which had stamped him as one of the best
whips at his university.

Soon they were in a large hall with a
broad staircase in the centre and doors on
either side. The place was en fête, and
the exuberant splendour of the 'spare no
expense' and 'leave it to the upholsterer'
style of furnishing was somewhat toned
down by the multitude of lovely ferns,
plants, and flowers with which the place
was adorned. An animated throng, which
filled the drawing-rooms and overflowed
into the hall, and the babble of many
tongues, proclaimed a large gathering and
spoke well for the hospitality of Wreford,
and the appreciation thereof on the part
of the country-side.

The Armers knew many of the guests,
and 'How d'ye do, Armer?' 'So glad
you've come, Miss Armer,' was heard on

every side, as Jack and his sister made
their way towards their hostess.

'I say, Nellie,' whispered Jack, 'how
shall we find the missus? we don't *know*
her?'

'Hush!' answered Nellie, 'here's one of
the daughters; it's the handsome, gushing
one. I must introduce you.'

'So *very* good of you to come,' gushed
the eldest Miss Denton, a large and exceedingly handsome damsel. 'Your brother?
yes? delighted, I'm sure. Are not we *too*
fortunate. Such a *heavenly* day! Flowers?
yes, dearest papa *dotes* on flowers. But I
forgot, you do not know mamma yet; she
is *dying* to know you;' and she led the way
into the drawing-room.

Piloted by the lovely Theresa, Nellie
and her brother were soon exchanging the
customary civilities with the mistress of
Wreford, and solving at the same time the
mystery of young Mr. Denton's extraction,
for that young gentleman 'favoured' his

mother, who was tall and thin, and of what the dressmakers call 'a genteel figure.'

Mrs. Denton was a very ambitious and a very determined woman ; it was through her efforts (and not, too, without painful pinching and screwing) that her children had obtained an amount of education which rendered them able to hold their own in the society to which the sudden change in the fortunes of the family gave them access. It was the aim and end of Mrs. Denton's life to climb up to the very topmost rungs of the social ladder, and with great wealth, an acute intelligence, and a large fund of persistence she did not despair of attaining this end. Mrs. Denton's father had been a chemist and druggist; he was well enough off to keep a servant-girl, and this gave his daughter an amount of time she would have found heavy upon her hands had it not been for the circulating library. Her mother had doted upon her daughter, and, an ignorant woman herself, regarded with something of awe Louisa's devotion to books.

Louisa spent all her time devouring novels, and many were the visions of aristocratic lovers, gorgeous establishments, liveried menials, and splendid equipages in which she indulged; but alas! for her dreams; time wore on, her mother was dead, her father was getting very old, and Louisa's 'genteel figure' was lapsing into the skinny stage, and still the aristocracy held aloof, and Louisa was fain to accept the respectful admiration of their neighbour and her father's friend, Henry Denton. It is a question, however, whether she could have brought herself to consent to such a total wrecking of all her castles in the air if it had not been for one fact. Mr. Denton had an only brother, some years older than himself. This brother, Benjamin Denton, had gone to Australia about the time when Henry was setting up (after due service and apprenticeship) as a grocer in the neighbourhood of Bloomsbury.

Benjamin Denton was a pushing, persevering, hard-working man, and after many years of self-denying labour he had amassed a considerable fortune. He married in the colony when he was already advanced in years, and brought his wife on a bridal trip to the mother country. Finding his brother comfortably settled in a flourishing business, he saw there was no need for the help he was perfectly willing to have given; and, making no parade of his wealth, he returned to Australia, after gladdening the hearts of his nephews and his nieces with handsome presents. Now, Henry Denton had heard from others of his brother's wealth, and Mrs. Denton in accepting Henry had her eagle eye on this money, of which the guileless Henry had often made boast in her father's parlour. Benjamin was not married nor likely to marry when the fair Louisa became

Mrs. Henry, and his marriage was a terrible blow to that covetous lady; but as the years went on, and no little Benjamins appeared, she learnt to endure the burden. Five years after Benjamin's wedding-trip his wife died, and having no one, now, upon whom he could bestow his affections he bestowed them upon his money, and for the latter years of his life he became almost a miser.

When Henry Denton's children became a great expense to their parents, he wished to apply to his wealthy brother to help in their education and setting out in life, but his wife would by no means allow him to do so. A wonderfully shrewd woman was Mrs. Denton. Still keeping up a friendly correspondence with her brother-in-law, she never once mentioned the word money, but she strained her resources to the utmost, and deprived herself almost of necessities, in order to fit her children for what must be their good fortune unless

Uncle Benjamin left his money to some charitable institution or other, a possibility which sometimes caused her secret panics of fear.

The result of this training on her children's part was that they utterly despised the shop, turned up their educated noses at their father's vulgarity, and made things altogether so unpleasant as to almost drive the good-natured little man to despair. But still the venerable Benjamin 'hung on,' and refused to retire from this world, and it became a serious question as to what was to be the outcome of this state of affairs. Many family discussions, not to say, quarrels, ended in the son, Henry, being articled to a solicitor (a 'genteel' profession) and the two girls getting situations as governesses, much to their discontent.

So things had gone on for some two years, when the news of Benjamin Denton's death came from Australia, and with the news Mrs. Henry's reward for her self-denial and forethought, for Mr. Benjamin Denton left a most enormous fortune to his brother, with injunctions to him to buy an estate in England, and 'found a family.' It was not long before the grocery business was disposed of, Wreford bought, the house built and fitted up 'regardless of expense,' and the Dentons emerged from their chrysalis state into the condition of very fine butterflies indeed.

Of course the country-side was all agog to see what manner of folk these new people were, who were building such a palatial edifice for their habitation, laying out such enormous sums of money, and generally dispensing what young Armer called 'the nickles,' with a lavishness which made the mouths of the parsons and squireens of those parts, together with the mouths of their wives and children, to water, and brought about a breaking of the tenth commandment, which was, to say the least of it, shocking. All sorts of rumours preceded the arrival and final settling in of the Denton family. Some said old Denton was a magnificent money-lender; others hinted at the three golden balls as the sign of his wealth; and some, with a side-glance at the Coombridge folk, spoke of the Stock Exchange; but one and all agreed that a mighty man of money was coming to live in their midst, and that it behoved them to receive him, and all his belongings, with open arms, with a view to the 'cakes and ale' which would probably be dispensed with no niggard hand.

The neighbouring clergy revolved dark schemes in their minds as to the restoration of their churches, and large subscriptions therefor, and their wives had sweet expectations as to annual donations to clothes, blanket, and coal clubs, while their daughters, together with all the other daughters of Eve 'in Society,' had pleasant visions of tennis-parties, dances, picnics, and other enlivenments of a dull

locality. It was known that there was an
only son, *unmarried*, and *some* ladies,
mothers and daughters too, nourished still
deeper designs in their chaste bosoms.

But although the clergy and the lesser
gentry had flocked to the gleaming portals
of Wreford in phaetons, wagonettes,
Stanhopes, shandrydans, and every im-
aginable vehicle, some bright and new,
but most of them second-hand, woebegone,
and shabby; though the neighbouring little
town of Bardon had sent, too, a noble
contingent in the shape of the two doctors
and the lawyer, and their respective wives;
though these devoted worshippers at the
shrine of Mammon had driven eight solid
miles up and down precipitous hills, and
over roads of a most astonishing badness;
though the heap of cards reached an
abnormal height, yet, still, to Mrs. Denton's
and her son's, and her two fair daughters'
deep disappointment and disgust, *the*
people of that division of the county had

failed to pay their devotions to the man of money, and were, indeed, conspicuous only by their absence.

In his secret heart, though he dared not to say so, the monied man himself was rather relieved than otherwise at this neglect on the part of what he called 'the nobs,' for he had serious misgivings as to how he should conduct himself in the presence of members of our noble British aristocracy, and, indeed, was what the country-folk around him would have called ' mazed ' with all this new magnificence. Secretly he often sighed for his snug parlour behind the old shop in Bloomsbury, with its balmy odours of cheese, bacon, coffee, &c., &c. He missed, too, the club of congenial spirits which assembled nightly in the public-house where he was wont of yore to spend his evenings, smoking the pipe of peace and partaking of the enlivening glass of gin-and-water ('Hot with; *two* lumps of sugar, and a slice of lemon, if you please, miss, *as* usual ') ; where also he was much looked up to, on account of the great reputed riches of his brother (a subject on which he frequently descanted), and his chance of one day succeeding thereto.

It was an affecting scene when he took a fond and last farewell of what his wife called 'his boon companions,' and stood 'glasses round' for the last time; and often, as he wandered aimlessly about his large domain, he sighed at the emptiness of riches, and in his heart almost envied the very servants who waited on him ; *they* had not got to mind their 'hs' to say nothing of their 'ps' and 'qs' generally. And it was not until he suddenly developed a strange and violent mania for orchids and hot-house plants that he found a modicum of peace, and began to enjoy his brother Ben's fortune.

CHAPTER III.

A SUDDEN ATTACHMENT.

THIS grand garden-party at Wreford was the first social shot of any calibre that the Dentons had fired off; such small fusilading as 'afternoon teas' they had ventured upon already, but this was the first big gun, and great had been the preparations and the anticipations thereanent. The social experience of the whole family was brought to bear upon this solemn function. Mr. Denton's experience was of the 'cress and shrimp,' or a 'bit of somethink 'ot,' order, so *his* advice was not of much use; but Mrs. Denton was learned in the noble works of fiction of the fashionable sort, and the Misses Denton had been in good situations, and had viewed the doings of the great from the vantage ground of the bannisters, to say nothing of being occasionally asked to 'come down after dinner.' No wonder, then, that Mrs. Denton's first 'at home,' though rather an omnium gatherum, was a great success.

No expense was spared, a string band from Plymouth discoursed sweet music, and a company of glee singers from the same place asked each other, in musical tones, questions as to the whereabouts of Sylvia, Chloe, and Lubin, exhorted one another to 'trip it like fairies,' and gave the amusing history of the gentleman who 'brewed good stingo,' and possessed a dog whose name was (most conveniently for the rhyme) Bingo. There was tennis for the young and agile, and croquet for those who preferred to amuse themselves less vigorously; the refreshments were, as the Bardon lawyer—an obese gentleman, reported to have seen 'life' in his youth, and of bibulous propensities—described them, 'First-class, champagne up to the masthead; give your orders, gents, the waiter's in the room.'

And if some of the guests, with reminiscences of the aristocratic meets of the county, turned up their noses at the exuberant joviality of the before-quoted lawyer and his friends, and wondered 'why Mrs. Denton had asked those horrible So-and-sos, and those too vulgar What'shis-names,' Mrs. Denton was very apt to take the hint which their contemptuous glances gave her, and began in her mind that very afternoon the process of weeding, which was, in course of time, to make it a privilege to be invited to Wreford, and a joy of the highest social flavour to be seen there.

'Well! I'm glad it's over,' said Mrs. Denton, with a sigh of relief, as she turned from the window whence she, with her interesting family, had been watching the last vehicle as it disappeared down the drive. 'I'm glad it's over, and I don't think it was bad for a first attempt.'

'For *my* part,' said Mr. Denton, 'I don't hold with these 'arf-an'-'arf affairs, as I call 'em; give me a good dinner-party, or a regular 'op. Seems so queer for the company to go just as they're a-gettin' comfortable together, and the smell of the dinner a-coming up the stairs. That ain't *my* idea of 'orspitality.'

'We must, however, conform to the usages of society,' said his son, who dropped his lisp in the bosom of his family, but who was apt to be Johnsonian in his periods, and was, truth to tell, something of a bore.

''Ang society!' said his father, 'I'm sick to death of the word. Society! society! all day long; why can't you be content with what you've got, and not go hankering after things you can't get?'

'My dear,' said his wife, 'I intend to

leave no stone unturned till we occupy the
position in the county to which our wealth
entitles us.'

'All I can say then, Louisa,' rejoined
her spouse, 'is, that you'll 'ave to turn
over a good many of 'em;' and, with
this parting shot, he went off to super-
intend the removal of some of his favourite
plants from the hall to their homes in the
hot-houses.

'Isn't it *too* dreadful, mamma, the way
father drops his "h's"? I declare, he gets
worse every day,' said Theresa.

'*I* believe he does it on purpose,' said
Emily.

'Well, my dears,' said their mother, 'I'm
sure I do all I can. I make him practise
every morning, when he is dressing. I
make him say sentences with quantities
of "h's" in them after me; but it isn't a
bit of good—he only laughs, and does it
worse than ever. He says, "He's too old
a dog to learn new tricks."'

'If he would only cease to persist in the pernicious habit of eating with his knife, it would afford me infinite relief,' remarked the long and magniloquent Henry. 'Yesterday, at dinner, I could see the men grinning, when he was trying to get peas into his mouth, and they kept running off the knife. It is a grievous trial.'

Here the conclave broke up, for the two sisters retired to indulge in their favourite pastime of bedizening their fair persons, leaving Henry and his mother together.

'Henry,' said Mrs. Denton, after a pause, during which she seemed to be deeply pondering over some weighty problem, 'did you notice those Armers? What do you think of them?'

Henry turned round from the window, whence he had been looking out, in the meanwhile, in an absent manner.

'Eh, mother? I beg your pardon. What was it you said?' he asked.

'I asked you what you thought of the Armers?'

'I think Miss Armer is quite the nicest girl I ever saw,' said Master Henry, naturally enough for once in his life, and naïvely ignoring the other members of the family in question.

Mrs. Denton gave a quick glance at him, and seemed considerably surprised at the unusual warmth with which her languid son spoke.

'Well, I must say I don't understand it at all,' she said. 'Mr. Armer's only a stockbroker, after all. They are not half as rich as your papa. I never heard they were much of it in the way of birth, and yet they seem to know everybody—Lord Limborne, the Holywells, the Portons: all the best people know them. I wonder why it is?'

'She is a most charming girl. The sweetest smile, the loveliest little hands and feet, and the most beautiful eyes I ever gazed upon—her figure is grace personified,' remarked Henry.

'Well! upon my word, Harry! If you ain't bewitched!' cried his mother, lapsing, in her astonishment, into the vernacular of her youth. 'What's come to the boy? Why, you've only seen her twice! What a way you do go on, Henry!'

'Mother,' said her son, in solemn tones, 'my mind is made up. I have met my Fate. Long, long have I foreboded it; and the future will be one long blank to me, if it be not shared with that divine girl. I know it seems strange to you, mother; but it is not strange to *me!* for I have long known that some such a fate was in store for me. I have long felt that I was marked out for gloom and sorrow;' and he sighed dismally.

'What nonsense you talk, Henry!' said Mrs. Denton. 'Why, *any* girl would jump for joy to get such a chance. I do hope this is only a passing fancy, for it is the

dream of my life for you to marry a title—
the Honourable Mrs. Denton, the Lady
Mary Denton,' repeated Mrs. Denton; and
she almost smacked her lips at the delicious sound.

'Nay, mother,' said Henry, who seemed
determined that 'Melancholy should mark
him for her own,' and who had, to tell
the truth, been 'going in for' an unwhole-
some course of Byronic literature. 'Nay,
mother, I shall wed with no one else;
indeed, I shall *never* know the joys of
domestic life; no children shall ever prat-
tle round these knees; no wife shall soothe
this aching brow, for she loves me not.
I can plainly perceive that she loves me
not.'

'She would be a most impudent young
hussy if she *did*,' said his mother, 'seeing
that to-day is only the second time she
ever set eyes on you. Come, Henry, don't
be a fool!' (for the weak-minded young
man was actually sobbing with self-pity)

E 2

'your old mother will help you, if you are
set upon the girl, though I must say it is a
bitter disappointment to me, for I *should*
have liked a titled daughter-in-law,' she
added, with a sigh; 'but,' she went on,
brightening up, 'after all, it is very sudden,
and, perhaps, you will see some one you
like better.'

'Never, mother, never!' said the doleful
Henry. 'I feel in myself that I am
destined to grief and sorrow.' And he
groaned in a dreadful and hollow way
which could only have come to him by as-
siduous practice; groans, indeed, which
would have 'brought down the house' in
any transpontine theatre.

'For goodness sake, Henry, don't make
such dreadful noises,' said his mother,
with a start at the dismal sound. 'I declare you make my flesh creep, going on
in that way. And there's the gong; yes,
it's half-past seven, and time to dress for
dinner. Don't you fret, Harry, it will all

come right enough, never you fear;' and kissing her son, whom she loved with a doting affection which could see no faults in him, Mrs. Denton hastened away to attend to her toilette for dinner.

Henry was standing, leaning against the mantel-piece, a picture of woe, when his father came bustling into the room.

'Been looking after the plants,' he said. 'Lazy lot of beggars them gardeners are, to be sure. If you want a thing done, do it yourself. Look 'ere! Look at my 'ands! black as yer 'at!' he was rambling on, when he caught a glimpse of his son's woe-begone visage. 'Ullo, 'Arry—I mean Harry! Why, what's the matter with you, my boy? You ain't taken nothing at the "Al Fresky," as I call it, that's disagreed with you, 'ave you? . . . Bless the boy! what a temper he's in, to be sure; he *must* have eat somethink,' he went on, as his son rushed by him, and strode haughtily across the hall on the way to his own room.

'Ah, well!' sighed Mr. Denton, his round and ruddy face looking quite dismal, 'Ben's money has turned 'em all topsy-turvy, and I almost wish I'd never seen the colour of it. Money ain't everything, after all. Now I must go and put on swaller-tails, I suppose. Well, perhaps I shall get used to it all some day; but just now I reglar hate all this humbug and show.' And, with another portentous sigh, the master of Wreford went to prepare for the greatest event of the day—to *him*, at least—his dinner.

Very soon after the Dentons' 'Al Fresky,' as the head of that family called their 'at home,' the Wreford barouche was seen winding its tortuous way up the Coombridge drive; a truly magnificent 'turn-out' it was, and more suited to the congenial locality of Hyde Park than to the steep and hilly roads of Devonshire. In the stony and rutty *by-ways* with which that county abounds, and which are a trial to horse-flesh, and even to the stoutest of shoe-leather, this resplendent equipage was a rank impossibility; but its appearance in the main roads was a constant joy to the rustic mind, which regarded with some-thing of awe its light yellow body, its brightly emblazoned and new (in more senses than one) coats-of-arms, the shining silver harness, and the gorgeous attire of the coachman and footman. Indeed, Mr. Lamacraft, who kept *the* village shop at Coombridge, and had been to London, and was much looked up to in those parts as a man who had seen the world—Mr. Lama-craft said,

"'Tis like the Lord Mayor's Show; not even him rode in a more bewtiful coach, for certain.'

The love-stricken Henry Denton would allow his mother no peace until she had made this pilgrimage (for he could not as yet summon up enough courage to go by himself), and he fronted his mother and his eldest sister Theresa in the carriage. But Mrs. Denton had other reasons besides her desire to please her son, which induced her to make this call. The pleasant and refined manners of the Coombridge folk, their well-known wealth, and the fact, perhaps, that they did not particularly care for the honour, and took no manner of means to force it upon themselves, had gained for them a footing in the county society, and Mrs. Denton saw in their friendship a considerable help towards the attainment of her ambitious designs. More particularly she wished through the Armers to get an introduction to Lord Limborne, whose place, Limborne Castle, was not very far from Wreford, and whose mother (for Lord Limborne was a bachelor) had not yet called upon her wealthy neighbours.

Fortune favoured Mrs. Denton; her visit was most opportune, for when the Wreford carriage, in all its glistening

beauty, drove up to the Coombridge front
door, Jack Armer was playing a single-
handed 'sett' at tennis on the lawn before
the house against his sister and Lord Limborne himself. As they descended from
their carriage, Nellie advanced to meet
her callers racket in hand, and looking a
perfect picture in her flannel tennis costume and Tam-o'-Shanter cap.

'Do not let us disturb your game, Miss
Armer,' said Mrs. Denton, as they shook
hands. 'I shall so much like to watch
you ; Theresa and I will sit under the
trees here, and Henry can help Mr.
Armer.'

Now his mother could not have done
Henry a worse turn, for he did not shine
as an athlete ; he abhorred all manner of
exercises, and never felt more truly at
home than when he was seated in his
luxurious arm-chair in his 'study' at
Wreford, surrounded with all the pet
fancies of the 'utterest' æstheticism, and

'studyiug' the last new novel or the latest
development of the fleshly school of
poetry.

'Jack will be delighted, I am sure,' said
Nellie, turning to Henry Denton, and
wondering how his weedy figure, correct
frock-coat, and stove-pipe hat would look
in the throes of 'vantage to us.'

'Really, Miss Armer,' said Henry, torn
between a desire to be near the object of
his affection, and a knowledge of his want
of skill and hatred of the game—'really I
am but a poor tennis-player, and I fear
your brother will not be too pleathed with
hith partner; but if *you* wish it . . .'

Just then Jack and Lord Limborne came
up, and when Nellie had introduced the
Dentons to Lord Limborne, and while they
were trying to make a good impression
upon 'his lordship,'

'Jack,' she said to her brother, 'do, for
goodness' sake, *make* the lithping æsthete
play; it will be *too* delightful! Think of

his coat-tails, his hat, and his long legs!'

'All right,' said Jack, 'we'll make him spin round, and give him a little "gentle exercise" for once in his life. I say, Denton,' he called out, 'come and take a racket. These two are too much for me; come and help me, there's a good fellow.'

'Yes, do, Mr. Denton,' Lord Limborne chimed in, catching a meaning glance from the mischievous Nellie, 'we are too many for Armer.'

Mr. Denton, junior, who 'loved a lord,' did not like to refuse Lord Limborne, and he desired above all things to 'get into the good books' of the fair Nellie; so, with many qualms as to what kind of an exhibition he was going to make of himself, he buttoned his frock-coat to his fragile form, fixed his tall hat firmly on his manly brow, and, grasping his racket with an air of stern determination, he prepared for the worst. Nor was this 'worst' long in coming upon him, for the three other players

combined to give him no rest; his partner,
making a huge pretence at action himself,
urged the unfortunate young man to continued exertions, while Nellie and Lord
Limborne so arranged matters for him
that his time was spent in frantic and
often fruitless runs after the ball from one
side of the court to the other. Unaccustomed as young Denton was to any exercise beyond a short walk, or a (not unfear-
fraught) amble upon a safe and easy cob,
the violence of his springs, jumps, and
short runs reduced him, in a very little
time, to a condition almost pitiable; the
perspiration simply rolled down his face,
which was heated to a fine purple colour;
the top button of his shirt had given way,
and allowed his collar to dangle gracefully
over his breast; he had lost his hat at an
early stage of the proceedings, and his
hair, usually sleek and lank, was in ad-
mired disorder. Altogether, when the game
was over, and his adversaries were pro-

claimed the victors, he presented an odd appearance as he stood gasping for breath and mopping his face with an elegant silk handkerchief.

'Have another sett, Denton,' said Jack. 'We'll beat them next time; you'll get into your "form," you know, after a sett or two.'

'Yes, do, Mr. Denton,' said Nellie, who, with her brother and Lord Limborne, looked as cool as the proverbial cucumber, and presented a refreshing contrast to the perspiring æsthete. 'Do have another game.'

'I think we'll change courts this time,' Lord Limborne joined in, following suit, and taking it as a matter of course that they should go on playing.

'I—ah—I don't think I will play any more, thank you,' said Henry Denton, inwardly resolving that not lords, nor even dukes or marquises, or love himself should persuade him to perform such another dance of death. 'I—ah—I have not played for some time, and the exercise ith a little thevere at first, don't you know. But perhaps my thithter will take my racket,' he added, with a vicious desire to make her a sharer in his sufferings. No persuasions could induce him to change his mind, or persuade the fair, elaborately-attired Theresa to risk the deranging of her elegant costume, so Nellie proposed that they should refresh themselves with afternoon tea. Mrs. Denton seized upon the opportunity to ingratiate herself with Lord Limborne, and she and her daughter kept up a running fire of the smallest of small talk with him, while Henry was unmercifully handled by Jack and his sister, though his conceit was of so thick and solid a nature that their sharp prongings failed to pass through it, and he did not even know that they were laughing at his manifold affectations, but rather thought he was making a good impression.

'Oh,' sighed Nellie, as, at last, the Dentons drove away, 'what a relief! I thought they never *would* go.'

'A regular visitation,' said Jack.

'Don't you adore Theresa, **Lord Lim-borne?**' asked Nellie.

'**I can** scarcely go so far as that **as yet,** this **is the first time I have met the** fair lady,' answered **Lord Limborne;** 'but **I think** *you* **have made a conquest, Miss** Armer; our long, æsthetic friend bestowed looks **full** of devotion **upon you, and went** into the most correct of Grosvenor Gallery attitudes, expressing attachment, humility in the presence of the **object of** devotion, and so **forth;** were all these **contortions** of body and visage wasted **upon you?'**

'I thought he **was** suffering from cramp, or something, after his **violent exertions.** That **game** was too lovely, **wasn't it, Jack?'** said Nellie.

'Well, **it serves** him **right,'** said Jack. 'I **hate a** fellow who moons about all day, and does nothing but attire himself in gorgeous raiment and reads novels. If he would go in for a daily course of tennis for a month, he would at least look wholesome, which he certainly does not at present.'

'I wonder what Lady Limborne will think of her neighbours? I suppose she will call,' said Nellie, looking at Lord Limborne.

'She has not said anything to me about it,' replied Lord Limborne, 'but I don't think my mother is likely to care much about their gilded magnificences of Wreford. I hear the father has difficulties with his " h's " and that kind of thing.'

'He is quite the nicest of them all, though he *does* call Wreford an "'ealthy 'ouse," and asks you to "come and 'ave a look at his 'ot-'ouses." There is no pretence about Mr. Denton, and I like him, and mean to be great friends with him,' said Nellie. 'Won't you stay and dine with us?' she went on, as Lord Limborne came forward to make his adieux; 'father will be so disappointed if he does not see you : he has gone to look after some new buildings on one of the farms, but he is sure to be in soon.'

'Of course you must stay, Limborne,' said Jack; 'come up to my room and shift.'

'It is very kind of you—I should like to stay of all things; there is no one at the Castle, and I feel like "Mariana in the Moated Grange" there. You must excuse "morning costume," Miss Armer,' said Lord Limborne.

'Oh, never mind that,' said Jack; 'we are not proud, and I shall be glad of the excuse to get out of the claw-hammer coat business, and keep you company.'

And the two friends went off to Jack's domains.

CHAPTER IV.

PLACE FOR HER LADYSHIP.

LORD LIMBORNE was glad of any excuse which gave him the chance of a few more hours in the company of Squire Armer's daughter; he had a decided liking for that fascinating young lady, and was beginning to hope that one day she would take up her abode at Limborne Castle as the lovely mistress thereof. There were, however, serious difficulties in the way, for his mother was the very incarnation of pride, and would have looked upon such a marriage as a decided *mésalliance*, in spite of Mr. Armer's reputed wealth, and the large share of it which was sure to fall to the lot of his only daughter. Lady Limborne had determined that her son should marry a lady possessing not only the attractions of wealth, but of rank also, and she was even now searching among her exalted connections and acquaintances for a suitable mate for the noble house of Limborne.

It was, indeed, necessary that the future Lady Limborne should have well-filled money-bags, for Lord Limborne was a poor peer, and Limborne Castle was a most expensive place to keep up. The late lord had been a quiet man, contented to live at home, and occupied in the arduous business of trying to make both ends meet; but, in spite of the strictest economy, these ends refused to respond to his strenuous efforts, and the later years of his life were darkened by the shadow of debts he could not help incurring, and which he saw no means of satisfying.

He had married early in life the daughter of a Scotch peer, as economical, but also, unfortunately, as poor as himself, but whose pedigree stretched back into quite mythic ages. An only child, the present Lord Limborne, had lost his father some six years ago. At the time of our story he was twenty-eight ; his mother perfectly idolised him, and that not without reason, for her son, besides being naturally of a kindly disposition, was a remarkably clever man, and one not unlikely to make his mark in the world.

Unlike Mr. Chamberlain's friends of what Jeames de la Pluche called the 'hupper suckles,' who 'Toil not, neither do they spin,' Lord Limborne had already toiled to some purpose, and spun with singular success. He had left Oxford with the highest of honours, and was already known as a rising man, and as the author of some pamphlets and articles on the 'burning questions' of the day, which had made no small stir.

In person he was tall and of good figure, and, though his face could scarcely be called a handsome one, yet there was an expression of power in his broad forehead and dark eyes which struck one at once, and called the attention from the ruggedness of his too pronounced features. He was dark in complexion, and his hair, which was thin and fine, was black.

Cold and distant as Lady Limborne was to all the world besides, she was affectionate to her son, and her acquaintances—for she was not the kind of woman to make *friends*—would have been astonished could they have known the depth of her feelings towards her only child.

Lord Limborne recognised, and valued at its proper high price, the affection of his mother, and he repaid her with a rare devotion. It was, therefore, with mingled feelings that he read a letter from Lady Limborne which he received on the morning after he had dined at Coombridge, and

which announced her arrival for that afternoon. On the one hand he was glad at
the thought of seeing his mother again
after what was for her a long absence,
and, on the other hand, his mother had
dropped many hints as to her object in
going amongst her connections in London once more ; he knew well enough that
she had set her heart upon his making
what she would look upon as a splendid
marriage, and he was dismally certain of
the disappointment she would feel, and no
doubt express, when she learnt that her
son had chosen for himself, and had fixed
his affections in a rank of life peculiarly
obnoxious to the proud Lady Limborne.

The contrast between the narrow means
at the Castle and the wealth and ease at
Coombridge had often formed a topic of
conversation with her, and she seemed to
find a kind of relief in inveighing against
the very modest display of (as she chose
to term them) 'those roturiers' and those

'nouveaux riches' at Coombridge Manor.
From his very childhood Lord Limborne
had been duly, and even to tedium, in-
structed as to the advantages of 'blood,'
and the pitiful and contemptible condition
of those unfortunate persons in whose
veins ran a vital fluid wanting in the
'blueness' which distinguished the blood
of the Limbornes and the Hautfords, to
which latter noble house Lady Limborne
had the priceless privilege of belonging.

From time to time the society papers re-
corded marriages which were 'arranged'
between some titled, long-descended, and,
possibly, poverty-stricken individual of one
sex, and some individual of the other who
was without much descent, save the common one from father Adam, but who rejoiced in much money in many satisfactory
investments, and which (*horribile dictu!*)
had been gained in trade.

Lady Limborne never missed the opportunity to 'point her moral, and adorn her

tale,' which such announcements afforded
her. If, as not unfrequently happened,
such alliances ended in an absence of
domestic bliss, and *sometimes* in disgraceful
exposés not unconnected with the Divorce
Court, she was able to deliver a strong
and eloquent lecture upon her favourite
subject, with the additional advantage of
'living examples.' From long years of
brooding upon this subject, it had gradually
assumed the proportions of a sort of monomania with her, while, perhaps not un-
naturally, the constant insistance on his
mother's part had ended by utterly weary-
ing Lord Limborne, and giving him the
suspicion of a bias towards the other side
of the question.

A strong Conservative as he was, and
seeing, indeed, nothing but ruin for his
class in particular, and revolution and
anarchy for his country at large, in the
rabid dreams of a communistic radicalism,
he was, at the same time, too wise not to

mark, and advance with the signs of the times; and he did not fail of seeing how the middle-class of Great Britain, with its enormous wealth and consequent power, *must*, as the barriers of aristocratic pride were weakened by the needs of families of rank, gain an entrance into the higher circles of 'society.'

Indeed, so accustomed was he among his own intimate friends to seeing such alliances as those his mother so fervently hated, that he gradually came to regard the matter in an entirely different light, and so it came to pass that he had no such prejudices as agitated his mother to fight against, when the *mignonne* beauty of Nellie Armer, and the many charms of her character, began to attract him; and as their friendship ripened into a certain degree of intimacy, and he found her able to understand and sympathise with his views and ambitions upon subjects in which even his mother herself could find no interest;

when he saw how proud and delighted Nellie was at his various successes as a politician and a man of letters, he very soon came to the determination that here was a woman who would (could he gain her affections) make him a tender and a loving wife, and at the same time be a true companion to him, and a help to him as he worked his way to the goal of his high ambitions.

Young as he was, Lord Limborne was already a man of mark, and there was nothing absurd in these ambitious dreamings of his; the lack of means was, of course, a great bar to his advancement, and, though he did not look to his possible alliance with the house of Armer as to a solution of *this* difficulty, at any rate it was evident enough that Nellie's father would be able to make *her* future secure, and to relieve her husband of fears in this direction.

Revolving these important matters in his mind, Lord Limborne was standing on the platform of the little wayside station some four miles from Limborne Castle. The train glided up, with the accustomed shrieking and scraping, and Lady Limborne was soon exchanging greetings with her son. Lord Limborne could see by her manner that his mother had important news to tell him; and he had an uneasy feeling as to what this news might be. Once seated together in the somewhat antediluvian Limborne carriage, which even the most careful of tendance could not redeem from a certain shabbiness, Lady Limborne opened her budget at once.

'You must be tired, mother,' said Lord Limborne. 'The carriage must have been like an oven.'

'Of course it was hot; but you know I do not feel the heat, James,' she replied; and, indeed, Lady Limborne looked, if one might apply such a homely comparison to so exalted a person, 'as fresh as a

daisy.' Tall and slight, with white hair
and blue eyes of the 'steely' order, with
high and somewhat pronounced features
of the clean-cut sort, supposed to belong
exclusively to 'persons of rank,' and called
'aristocratic,' Lady Limborne was the ideal
'haughty dame.' Her face was always
pale, and in moments (very rare) of excitement assumed a dead-white hue. She
was immensely proud of her hands, which
were, indeed, models of shapeliness, and
were, according to her views, the plain
evidences of her high descent and 'blue
blood.'

'I do not feel the heat, James, as you
know,' she said. 'There was, however,
a person in the carriage who looked so
offensively hot that I was obliged to call
Cerise, and have my things taken into
another carriage. Such people ought to
travel second-class.'

'My dear mother,' said her son, 'I
verily believe you would like to have the

sumptuary laws re-inforced : have different costumes for every class, and generally go back into the old days of feudalism, villeinage, and so forth;' and he smiled at what he called prejudice in his mother, but what would have looked to him remarkably like snobbism in any other person.

'I *do* think it would be an excellent thing if people could be made by law to keep in their proper positions,' rejoined Lady Limborne. 'But I have too much to tell you to talk about such matters now ;' and here she began a long account of her month's experiences, the people she had seen, the news of her coterie, and the various items of intelligence which she thought would interest her son.

During the delivery of this long monologue, Lord Limborne heard, with something of amusement and a certain amount of perturbation, frequent mention of a Lady Beldon (a high and mighty friend

of the family) and her daughter Emily;
and, as his mother went on with her
narration, he began to plainly perceive
that this Lady Emily Beldon was the
happy individual Lady Limborne had
selected for the high position of mistress
of Limborne Castle.   He was, therefore,
relieved when the carriage drew up under
the portico of the castle, and when, after
a few words, his mother left him, to relieve
herself of her travelling attire and of the
dust which had had the unconscionable
insolence to cleave to, and annoy, her
magnificence of Limborne.

Limborne Castle was a splendid home
for a gentleman of large means, but an
intolerable incubus to a poor man, such
as was the present owner.   It was a 'real,
bona-fide castle,' and no stucco imitation,
and the ancient towers still lorded it over
the huge edifice, part of which was, alas!
only too evidently going fast to decay.
As yet, however, the neglect, which Lord

Limborne's **small means and** his **father's** before him **had rendered a** sad **necessity,** had not gone far enough to be irremediable, and the enchanter's wand of wealth would soon make Limborne Castle what **it was in** olden days, one **of** the finest and most important seats **in** the beautiful county of Devon. However pressed he had been, the late **lord had** religiously avoided felling any **of the** timber, and the lordly groups of trees **in** Limborne **Park were still a** sight which people came from far and **near to** look **upon.** Within, many of the rooms were **left to** the dust and the spiders, for the establishment was necessarily **a** small one, and quite unable to cope with so large a number of rooms ; while the apartments occupied by **Lord** Limborne and **his** mother were furnished with chairs, settees, and sofas dingy as to their coverings, and *some* **of** them **not too** firm upon their venerable and **worm-eaten legs ;** the **win-**dow-hangings and carpets also bore plain marks of the hand of time, and the whole effect was dismal and depressing to the last degree. This fact seemed to be strongly borne in upon Lady Limborne as she sat in the drawing-room on the evening of her return home. Lord Limborne was leaning against the mantelpiece, thinking, to tell the truth, about Nellie Armer, and wondering (should she accept him) how his mother would 'take it.'

'Coming home fresh from some of the prettiest rooms in London, the general shabbiness of things here is most depressing, James,' she said. 'This old furniture is so much nicer than the gaudy modern stuff one sees, and is, indeed, quite priceless now this rage for Chippendale, Sheraton, and that sort of thing has risen ; a very little money would make these rooms perfect. Is there no possibility of spending a little here ?'

'I am sadly afraid not, mother,' answered Lord Limborne ; ' you know that two of the farms will be vacant soon, and I fear we shall have to do a great deal to them before we can get tenants.'

'But, James,' persisted Lady Limborne, 'I thought you were getting money for those articles you have been publishing; a hundred pounds even would make a great difference.'

'Ah! but, my dear mother,' said Lord Limborne, with a weariful sigh, 'a great many more hundreds than I am afraid I can earn by my pen are, as you know, absolutely *needed* here on the estate, and things are not so well with farmers as they were of old. I fear the rents *must* go down.'

'Then you must borrow again, James dear, I suppose,' she said, with an anxious look at her son. 'Can't *anything* be done to avoid new debts?'

'No, mother, I am afraid we must borrow, though heaven knows! there is enough on the land already. We cannot let the farms without spending money on them, they are in shocking repair; one of the out-going tenants is a widow, and I can't be hard on her, and the other is that good-for-nothing fellow at Beer, and he is absolutely penniless. I have neither the capital nor the inclination to farm the land myself, and, of course, we can't do without the rents, and let the farms lie fallow. But,' he added, after a pause of anxious thought on the subject, 'I did not mean to worry you, mother, particularly on this the very first night of your coming home.'

'James,' said his mother, solemnly, 'I am glad the subject has been broached, for it makes it more easy for me to say to you what I am going to say. There is only one way out of all these miserable difficulties, which, sad as they are, are not so unbearable to me as the thought of my son with his talents wasted and his future ruined. There is only one way; I have

felt this all along. James, you must do
what I have so frequently urged upon you,
you must seek an alliance where you can
have the two so necessary advantages of
rank and money. I have no doubt you
could easily enough get the latter, for
there must be numbers of rich people of
low birth who would be glad to gain for
their daughters such a position as your
wife would hold; but I am sure my lessons
have given you a just horror of such
mésalliances. One of my objects in leaving
home was that I might seek among our
own people one who should combine the
advantages I spoke of ; and, James, I feel
sure you will be glad to hear I have found
a girl who is in every way suited to the
position, and who has the means to relieve
you from these sordid embarrassments, and
help you in your career.'

'But, my dear mother,' said Lord Limborne, laughing, 'in what a cold-blooded
way do you dispose of me! One cannot

marry to order,—we are not living in France; and, moreover, the young lady in question, whoever she may be, *might* not see the advantages of this position of mine in quite the same light as it presents itself to you. And, besides, I am not so fatuous as to believe that a girl has only to regard my attractive person and physiognomy to, at once, fall violently in love with me, and to offer to pour her millions into my meagre account with the Exeter bank. Neither am *I* in the state of mind in which Punch's housemaid found herself, "of that 'appy disposition as she could marry *any* man." It is possible the girl you speak of may not appear to me in the golden light in which you seem to regard her.'

'My dear James,' said his mother, with a reproachful look, 'I am sorry to hear you talk in this light manner of a matter of such importance. People in our position and rank of life do not choose . their husbands and wives in the happy-go-lucky fashion of the lower orders.'

'Nay, mother,' interrupted Lord Limborne, still refusing to discuss the match seriously, 'I am given to understand that these same folk of whom you speak *do* use an amount of circumspection in this matter which custom denies us. The beneficient institution of "keeping company" gives them an opportunity of knowing each other's little peculiarities before such a serious undertaking as a regular engagement, and the housemaid in question will probably have gone through a long and exciting course of "young men" before she settles her affections for good and all. I am seriously thinking of commending to the Lords a proposal for leasehold engagements of one, two, or three months, renewable at the expiration of the first and second months at will. It would go far to do away with breach of promise cases.'

'If you will insist on talking in this

ridiculous manner, I think I had better
leave you,' said Lady Limborne, offended
at her son's light tone.

'I did not mean to offend you, mother,'
he said, 'but, seriously, I am not thinking
of making a dowager of you just at present, and——'

'But, James,' she interrupted, 'what
time could be better than the present? I
heard, and was proud to hear, frequently
of you in high quarters, your name is
very much spoken of, and, if you only
had means, you would be certain of advancement. Lord Beldon spoke most
highly of your services to the party, and
Lady Beldon is very well disposed towards you. It is no use disguising the
matter. I have hinted very plainly to Lady
Beldon my hopes as regards you and her
daughter, and I think I may assure you
that you will be received there as you
ought to be received. There is, I took
the pains to discover, no one in your way,

and I believe a very little trouble on your part would secure Emily.'

Lord Limborne had been restlessly striding across and across the room whilst his mother made this very plain exposition of her views matrimonial as concerning her son and the fair Lady Emily, and, as she paused in her narration, he stopped, and said, slowly,

'I am, indeed, sorry you have taken so much trouble, and I regret extremely that you should have ever *hinted* at such a thing to any of the Beldons. I am sorry to have to disappoint you, mother; you should, at least, have consulted with me first. I have not the slightest suspicion that Emily Beldon has ever given the faintest thought to me, and I declare to you, solemnly, that if she loved me to distraction,—a highly improbable state of affairs,—I should most certainly never think of marrying *her*.'

'James, I trust you will think better of

this,' said Lady Limborne, in the coldest tones she had ever used to her son ; 'otherwise, you will place your mother in a most painful position, and that, too, with some of her oldest and best friends. You surely forget when you say, "I should have spoken to you before." I *did* speak of this to you, and you certainly did not answer me then as you answered me just now.'

' Well, mother, I remember now you *did* say something about it before you went away, but I had no idea you seriously meant it; I treated the matter as a jest, if you remember.'

' I do not think I will talk on this subject any more, at least at present. I think I will say good-night, I am tired, and this is a great trouble to me;' and Lady Limborne rose.

'Nay ; but, my dear mother, do not be angry with me, I will do anything you wish in any matter but this; it is surely reasonable that I should choose my own wife ?' and with this Lord Limborne went up to his mother, and kissed her. Lady Limborne received the salute with un- mistakeable coldness, and retired with much stateliness, thus leaving her son, who had opened the door for her, and who gazed after her with a puzzled and withal a sorrowful look.

As he smoked a solitary cigar in his own rooms before 'turning in,' he review- ed his position, and recognised with pain the struggle he should have to sustain with his proud and determined mother before she would give up her plans for him, and the still more bitter contest he should have to pass through before she would accept *his* plans for the future; he saw, too, that even if Nellie were willing to take him 'for better, for worse,' she was not the kind of girl to enter a family against the will and wish of the chief members of that family, and that she would most certainly refuse to listen to him, at whatever cost to her own and to his feelings, if he asked her to marry him against Lady Limborne's wish. How to keep the knowledge of Lady Limborne's opposition from Nellie, how to overcome these rooted prejudices of his mother's, how to reconcile her to her disappointment anent the Beldons—these were questions which kept him up far into the balmy summer night, and gave him but little rest even when at last he 'denuded himself of his outer integuments,' or, to put it more plainly, undressed himself, and got into bed.

CHAPTER V.

TAKING HIS DEGREE.

Miss Helen Armer had a very shrewd suspicion that she was not unpleasing to his lordship of Limborne, and, even if she had had no such suspicions, her brother Jack's gibes at her would very soon have aroused them. When they were alone together, he would call her 'my Lady,' and 'your Ladyship,' and would treat her with an absurd and burlesque affection of respect.

Lord Limborne was fond of Jack Armer, he liked his easy-going good nature, and his constant flow of good spirits was a refreshment to Lord

Limborne, who had many troubles to make
him grave enough, and who was, indeed,
naturally of a somewhat grave disposition.
He had never confided his feelings for
Nellie to her brother, for his self-contained
character did not tempt him with the
desire for confidantes usually so common
under such circumstances.

It is, indeed, refreshing, though occasionally wearisome, to listen to the fond
declamations of the enamoured, and the
man who has 'passed through the fire,'
and has been fortunate enough to have
escaped with but little of hurt, must be
amused considerably at the redundancy of
superlative, the piled-up 'derangement of
epitaphs,' with which fond youth is wont
to extol 'the only woman he ever loved.'
Such glowing descriptions, clad in such
fanciful language did the evil-minded Jack
pour into his devoted sister's ears as the
utterances of the lovelorn Limborne, for
Master Jack was charmed with this chance

of turning the tables upon Nellie, and he took a huge delight in the novel exercise, and repeated his doses 'ad nauseam.' The attentions, too, of the ridiculous Henry Denton did not escape the astute young man, as he failed not, *too* frequently, to impress upon his sister.

Not a week passed without the appearance of one or other or both these two so opposite admirers, and it needed all the young lady's powers of repartee, which were considerable, to enable her to parry Jack's constant attacks, and she must have possessed a most angelic patience, or she would long ago have been really angry with her brother. Nellie was, however, too fond of Jack ever to be angry with him, and she hurled the lovely Theresa Denton at his head with immense effect, little knowing the fell designs which were stirring in the brains of that beauteous young lady and her ambitious mother.

Nellie was pleased, therefore, when the

important event in Jack's academical career took the small family to Cambridge, in order that the squire should see 'what he had got for his money,' for this created a diversion from a *taquinage* which was rapidly becoming monotonous. The modest position which young Armer's name filled at the tail-end of a third class among the ordinary degrees had been exalted by him to an undue eminence, and his father was expecting something of awe and majesty to surround this important end of nearly four years' study (?) His astonishment was therefore great at the disgusting exhibition of rowdyism which certain of the undergraduates seem to consider to be *de rigueur* on these occasions, and he very speedily conducted his daughter from the senate-house, and, at the same time, from the too conspicuous gallantry, or—to call it by its right name—the painful vulgarity of admiring swains in the gallery, who had 'spotted' her primrose-coloured costume, and had made complimentary, but decidedly embarrassing, remarks upon its beauty, and the still greater beauty of its fair wearer.

'Abominable set of young cubs!' exclaimed the squire, in a white heat of rage, as Jack in his cap and gown, and with the additional advantages of a 'white choker,' and the distinguishing B.A. 'strings,' followed them out, rejoicing in the dignity of his new academical status. 'Abominable set of young cubs! They ought to be flogged! Never heard such impertinence! "Him with the red face!" "Father of she!" (for the squire had not himself escaped without a few compliments). 'Upon my word, Jack, if I had known what an intolerable set of young cads you were living amongst, you should never have gone there. Never heard such a row in my life; it's disgraceful!'

'My dear father,' said Jack, indignantly, standing up for his order, 'you are a little *too* hot upon them . . . .'

'Not at all! not at all!' interrupted the squire, still bubbling over with rage.

'They don't mean anything offensive, I assure you,' Jack went on; 'they mean it as a compliment, don't you know.'

'Pretty compliment!' exclaimed his father. 'Red face, indeed!'

'Oh! father, I verily believe you are getting vain in your old age; your face *is* red,' laughed Nellie, 'you *know* it is; it is the dearest old face in the world, and, if we were not in the street with such a crowd, I should like to kiss it. Come, now, father, they are but boys after all . . . .'

'Oh! thank you, Miss Methusalem!' said Jack, scornfully.

'*You*, Jack,' said Nellie, with much solemnity, 'are a Bachelor of Arts, and, I am sure, you are *far* removed from the follies of impetuous youth.'

' And *you*, my lady,' whispered Jack, ' are of far too exalted a rank for a poor commoner to argue with, and I humbly beg your ladyship's pardon ;' and Jack took off his cap with a mighty sweep, and performed a stagy reverence, greatly to his father's astonishment, who thought he must be saluting some high university potentate, and who removed his own ' bell-topper,' with a sincere though less exaggerated politeness, hugely to Jack's delight.

' Oh ! this is, alas ! *too* much !' exclaimed that ingenuous youth, as they strolled along the King's Parade after the ceremony(?) ' This is *quite* too much !'

' What *do* you mean, Jack ?' asked the astonished Nellie, while her father looked questioningly at Jack.

' Why, *this*,' answered Jack, in a whisper, as Henry Denton presented himself before them, and came forward to greet them.

' Mr. Denton ?' said the squire, with a note of interrogation in his voice. ' Why,

I didn't know *you* were a Cambridge
"man," as Jack calls it, though "boy"
is a more just description after this morning's din.'

'You are quite right, Mr. Armer, I am
not a *Cambridge* man,' said Mr. Denton, as
he shook hands, placing a sort of accent
on 'Cambridge,' as if he might be an Ox·
ford, or a Heidelberg, or a Dublin man.
'I . . . ah . . . thought I would just
run down for a day or two, and . . . ah
. . . see the architecture, and . . . ah
. . . . that thort of thing, don't you
know. So glad I have happened to meet
you.'

Mr. Denton's sudden appearance was so
evidently intended, that Nellie, knowing
only too well the reason thereof, felt
somewhat embarrassed, while Jack, who
was also in the secret, was amused, and
not a little indignant at the same time,
for he decidedly did *not* approve of Henry's
'addresses.'

Mr. Armer, who frankly detested the Denton faction, and most particularly abominated the limp æsthete, frowned portentously at first at the happy (?) *rencontre;* if he had known as much as his son and his daughter knew, he would, not improbably, have 'said something,' something pretty strong, too, for the squire would have regarded young Denton's persistent persecution of his daughter as an unwarrantable impertinence, and, being a gentleman of a choleric habit, he would most likely have expressed this opinion in quite the plainest English. As it was, he looked upon the enamoured Henry simply as upon a neighbour; a most unpleasant one, certainly, but one whom it behoved him to be civil to *as* a neighbour.

'Come to do the lions, eh?' said the squire. 'Well, we are putting up at the " Bull," and are just going in to lunch ; you had better come in with us, and have something to eat.'

'Alack! and well-a-day!' sighed Jack, in a whisper to Nellie.

'I shall be charmed,' said the infatuated youth, with a most sheepish glance at Nellie, which glance Jack did not fail to mark and mimic.

For two whole days did Mr. Henry Denton bestow his valuable and entertaining company upon the unwilling Armers, to their huge disgust.

'I can't stand this any longer,' said Mr. Armer, on the afternoon of the second day. 'If I am compelled to be with that young man much longer, I shall be reduced to a wafer; I feel as if I had lost *pounds* since we met him. Why can't he speak like other people; that lisp of his drives me to distraction. And what on earth do *I* care about all this twaddle of art, china, poetry, and rot? Jack and [Nellie, I shan't stand it any longer; I shall go to town on my way home to-night.'

'I shall be only too glad to come with

you, father,' said Nellie, with a sigh of infinite relief. 'Of course, *you* can't, Jack, because you have "wines," and things to go to. I hope you are not "taking to drink."'

'You are talking about what you don't understand, young woman,' said Jack, 'and I shall treat your ignorant remarks with the silence they deserve.'

Nellie made a mouth at him, and ran upstairs gleefully, to get ready to depart. She had good reason to be relieved at the thought of leaving Cambridge, for her stay there had been rendered almost disgusting to her by the twaddlesome and sickly attentions of the devoted Henry.

Delighted at the chance of 'having the field to himself,' that infatuated young man would take no hint, no snubbing seemed to be of any use, though Nellie was well able to give, and *did* give him some very pronounced specimens of her ability in that way. He still tottered on the verge of proposing without actually committing himself, and giving Nellie an opportunity to refuse him, and be rid of him definitely.

'It wath to thee you, Mith Armer, and not the lionth that I came,' he had observed the day before, when he had caught her alone for a minute or two.

This was a little *too* much for Nellie, who lost her temper, and was most unequivocably rude to her adorer.

'Then, Mr. Denton,' she had answered, with much asperity, 'I consider it most impertinent of you to follow me about in this ridiculous way, and I must beg of you to let this be the last time you behave in so absurd a manner.'

This plain language rather startled the heir of Wreford, but not for long, for he quickly regained his accustomed fatuity, and made some original remarks about 'poles' and 'loadthstones,' and other electrical arrangements; to which remarks, it is needless to say, Nellie made him no

manner of reply.   It seemed impossible to
convince this young man that the whole
available feminine world was not pining
for the chance of one day sharing the
magnificence and the wealth of Wreford,
and at last, in despair, Nellie asked her
brother to help her.

'Jack,' she said the afternoon before,
when she had just given her would-be
lover the before-mentioned 'taste of her
quality,' and as, leaving Henry Denton to
the tender mercies of her father, she was
strolling about in one of the college gar-
dens, listening to the band and looking at
the folk who 'assisted at' a promenade
concert—'Jack, Mr. Denton, junior, is the
most jelly-fishy young man 1 have ever
had the misfortune to meet.'

'What is the matter with the æsthete
now? and why jelly-fishy?' asked Jack.

'He's so . . . so . . . it's not a very
nice word, but it just expresses him, he is
so flabby, Jack. If you prong him, he

closes up again, and there is no sign where the prong went in.'

' An apt simile, madam, and an elegant one for a young lady,' said Jack.

' But seriously, Jack, I wish you would help me. You know you often chaff (no, that is slang, and will not please your eminence), *laugh* about . . . well, about . . . pah! it's horrid even to say it . . . about me and Mr. Denton—there! Well, Jack, he is *too* dreadful, and I can*not* bear it any longer; he *sickens* me. He had the impertinence to say just now that he came down here to see *me.* Impudence!' said Nellie, stamping her little foot; ' and it's not a bit of use, he won't take even the *plainest* hint.'

' Well, but why don't you tell him to go? Say you won't have the article at any price.'

' How can I, Jack, when he hasn't asked me?' and Nellie sighed as deep a sigh as was ever breathed by love-sick damsel.

'Why, Nellie,' said Jack, with some amusement, **though** he was angry enough with the faithful Henry, **'you** sigh **as if** you *longed* for him to propose.'

' Of course I do; that **is the** very thing I *do* long **for, then** 1 **could** refuse him point-blank. **But,'** she added, **after a** pause, 'on second thoughts I don't be- lieve he would **give it up** even *then;* he is so densely conceited.'

'I'd gladly **help you** if I could,' **said** Jack; ' but what **on** earth can **I** do?'

'Can't you just tell him how I *hate* **him**? Now **do'ee, Jack** dear,' she **said,** in a wheedling tone.

'You bloodthirsty young woman, **you** most un-Christian female, how **can you,** brought up **in the** strictest principles of religion, hate your neighbour **in this** fero- cious way?' said Jack. 'However, **the** fellow *is* a fearful **bore**; he doesn't deserve any pity, and **I'll** do what **I** can for you. Here's father with old Blower,' he went

on, as the squire hove in sight with the
Reverend Blower in tow. 'I know that
dear coach of mine not wisely, but too
well, so I'm off,' and Jack suited his actions
to his words, and incontinently disappeared.

Jack Armer had no chance of giving
the amorous Denton what would doubtless
have been a very broad hint at Cambridge;
for as soon as Denton heard, at their
hotel, of the departure of Mr. and Miss
Armer, he incontinently ceased his studies
of architecture, and returned home. Now,
though Jack had laughed at his sister's
perturbation, he had remarked the pronounced and slightly snobbish nature of
the æsthetic young man's attentions, and
he was quite prepared to pour out the
vials of his wrath upon the offender's
head, and was proportionately disappointed to find, on inquiry at the 'Hoop,' (where
Denton was putting-up,) that he was gone.

'Never mind, young man,' said Jack to

himself, apostrophizing the absent Denton. 'Never mind! A time *will* come! I suppose young Blue China has followed them to Devonshire. Upon my word, it is too sickening; and, if it were not for my Degree Dinner to-morrow night, I would go home now, and indulge myself in the luxury of giving him a bit of my mind. However, he can't do much harm in a couple of days, and I'll make up for lost time, when I *do* see him;' and Master Jack departed on his pleasant business of looking up his old friends, and rejoicing with them over his extraordinary luck in 'rooking the examiners.'

Old Mr. Denton was standing at the hall-door at Wreford as his son got off the dog-cart, for which he had telegraphed, and which had accordingly met him at the nearest station to Wreford.

'Well, Henry,' said his father, 'you ain't had a very long outing. I didn't expect to see you home again so soon.

Your mother said you was going to 'ave a reglar turn at the antiquities of Cambridge, and 'ere you are, 'ome again before you can wink your eye, as the sayin' is. Well, I'm glad to see you back again, anyhow;' and he shook hands with his son and heir. 'I never could see,' he went on, 'the joke of starin' at mouldy old buildings myself—— Why! what's the matter now? You're always a-rushin' about, and a-interruptin' of your father. 'Enry, it ain't respectful, and I won't 'ave it;' and his round, good-natured face looked quite wrathful.

'I beg your pardon, I'm sure, father,' said Henry. 'I was hurrying in to see mother.'

'All right, my boy,' said his father, rapidly regaining his normal good-nature, and smiling. 'You'll find 'em in your mother's boodoor, though why she should call her parlour by such a outlandish name is beyond me; it's the fashion, I suppose. Yes, they're in the boodoor—leastways, your mar and Tresa—having a out and-out-palaver. Somethin' secret, you know; for they wouldn't let me come in just now. I wonder what they're up to *now*. Not another al fresky, I hope. When you've done with your mother, I want you to come over the 'ouses. I've got some real beauties out now;' and the old gentleman trotted off to his favourite plants and flowers.

Mrs. Denton and her daughter were indeed holding a most important conversation, and one which embraced a no less serious question than the settlement in life of the young lady.

'I sent your father away, Theresa,' Mrs. Denton began, as soon as the door closed upon her obedient spouse, 'because he, unfortunately, is lacking in the delicacy which the subject I asked you to come here and speak about demands.'

'Good gracious, ma!' exclaimed Theresa,

betrayed into vulgarity by her astonishment. 'Whatever do you mean?'

'My *dear* Theresa, you should not say "good gracious!" I am astonished at you, after all the expense of your education, when we had to pinch for it too.'

'Oh! never mind. You startled me. What is it, mamma?'

'Now, I want you to listen to me seriously, my dear. You know my only wish now is to see my children suitably settled in life. I mean, of course, married to people in the rank of life and the position which our wealth leads us to look for.'

'My dear mamma,' said Theresa, 'you need not say anything about *that*. I don't think that either I or Emily are at all likely to make a *mésalliance*.'

'Can't you guess, Theresa, at what I am thinking of?' said Mrs. Denton, with a searching look at her daughter.

'No, I don't in the least know. Do,

for goodness sake, stop this mystery, and tell me what you mean.'

'Goodness sake! Theresa,' murmured her mother, reproachfully.

'Oh! bother, mother. I'm sure you're enough to provoke a saint this evening. Whatever *is* the matter?'

'Nothing *is* the matter, my dear, but a great deal *may* be,' was the oracular reply.

'Well, I wish you would make haste, and not go on in this Guy Fawkes kind of way,' said the daughter, impatiently, and with a touch of her father's fertile imagery.

'Theresa,' said Mrs. Denton, solemnly, 'did you notice anything at Coombridge the other day?'

'Coombridge?—no, nothing particular, except the masculine costume of that Miss Armer; I must say I think the way girls dress like men, and play at all their games now-a-days, is horrid.'

Miss Denton was of a large order of architecture, and not likely to shine in a short tennis costume.

'Never mind about her just now,' Mrs. Denton went on. 'Did you notice anything about Lord Limborne? there!'

'Anything about Lord Limborne? Why, we've regularly talked him over since we met him, and I've said all I have to say on that subject already.'

'Well, I have *not*, Theresa,' said Mrs. Denton. 'I watched him, and I feel sure you have made a good impression in that quarter, my dear. The more I think of it, the more convinced I am that you have every chance of one day being Lady Limborne.'

Now, truth to tell, Theresa had been thinking the very same thing herself, and, though she had failed to remark the 'attentions' her mother's eagle eye had discovered, she had come to the same conclusion as that lady, and did *not* see why she should not be Lady Limborne; nevertheless, she kept these cogitations to herself, and affected a great surprise.

'*Me* . . . Lady Limborne!' she cried. 'My dear mamma, whatever could have made you think of such a thing as that? I'm sure I never . . . .'

'Well; but, Theresa,' interrupted her mother, 'I do not see anything at all astonishing or unlikely in the matter. Though I say it as shouldn't, anyone can see you are handsome enough, and every day people of title marry into money; and I confess I don't see why, with your looks and your Uncle Benjamin's fortune, you, and Emily too, should not marry a person of rank. I've set my heart on it, Theresa,' she went on, earnestly, 'and I can't tell you how disappointed I am at Henry's ridiculous fancy for that little Miss Armer.'

'*I* can't make out what he sees to like in her,' said Theresa; and, as a matter of fact, sisters very seldom *can* make out

what their brothers can see in *that* Miss
So-and-so; moreover, Theresa had a dawning feeling of dislike born of jealousy towards Nellie Armer—a dislike, indeed,
which after events nursed into downright
hatred.

'I can't see much in her myself,' rejoined Mrs. Denton; 'but you know what
Henry is—he *will* have his way, with all
his soft manners, and I suppose we must
make the best of it. But, as I was saying, if *Henry* disappoints me—I say *me*,
because your poor father would not care
if you all married carpenters and cook-
maids; nothing ever *will* bring that man
to a proper sense of his position. I declare
it is sometimes more than I can bear the
way he goes on; the familiar way in which
he talks with the servants is really *too*
shocking. But, what was I saying? for
when I get on the subject of your father
I quite lose myself—oh, about Henry. If
Henry *does* disappoint me, there is no

reason why one of you, or even both of you, should not be Lady Something or other.'

'But I don't see, mamma, *how* we are to, unless we are asked, and there aren't many lords about here.'

'Oh, you'll be asked quick enough, my dear; and when we are launched into society, and occupy our proper sphere, there will be plenty of lords glad enough of the chance to get one of the rich Mr. Denton's daughters, never fear. I don't mean to stay mewed up at Wreford all my life. But . . . who's there?' she called, as the handle of the door turned. 'Why, it's Henry!' she said, as she heard his voice, and hastened to unlock the door. 'We did not expect you home so soon, Henry,' she said, as she received his filial greeting; 'we were astonished to get your telegram.'

'You don't look like a conquering hero, Henry,' said Theresa, who knew her brother's reason for going to Cambridge, and spoke with a slight sneer. 'Weren't the Armers there, after all?'

'The Armers *were* at Cambridge, Theresa,' answered Henry. 'I do not know what I may resemble, but I think I have gained considerably by my journey. They all seemed glad to see me,' continued this obtuse individual. 'I may say their reception of me was most cordial, and I do not mind telling you, mother, that I was able to speak rather plainly to Nellie, and, though she seemed surprised at first, I have no doubt I shall succeed with perseverance.'

'I should think so,' said his fond parent. 'Why shouldn't you? It is not every girl who has such a chance offered her.'

'But, Henry,' said Theresa, 'you don't mean to say you have *proposed?*'

'No,' answered the infatuated one, 'I have not exactly proposed; but I have plainly let her see what I mean, and I have every hope of one day winning that charming and beautiful **girl.**'

Here Miss **Denton** positively sniffed, and, laughing contemptuously, she flounced out of the room.

'What *is* the matter with Theresa, mother?' asked Henry, astonished; 'her conduct is absolutely **vulgar.**'

'She **has been** put **out with** something or other,' said Mrs. Denton, who **was not** without **a certain** sympathy with **her** daughter in her sentiments as to the question **of** Nellie Armer. '**And** now, Henry, you have only just time to dress, **the first gong** sounded a long while **ago**, and **I** must be quick too;' and, with a smile at her **son**, Mrs. Denton effected her escape, **for she did** not particularly care for the flood **of love-**sick rhapsody which her *tête-à-têtes* with Henry usually brought **down upon her** devoted head.

CHAPTER VI.

A VERY PRETTY QUARREL.

'NELLY,' said Mr. Armer, senior, one morning about a week after their hasty retreat from Cambridge, 'just listen here a moment; here's a letter from Gidley, he says, "As I wish to consult you about those" . . . h'm . . . h'm . . . h'm . . . (business, my dear), "and more particularly wish to see my god-daughter Nellie, I shall, if you can put me up, run down to Devonshire for two nights the day after to-morrow." Why, that will be to-morrow, Nellie !' cried the squire, with just a suspicion of disgust in his voice.

'Yes, father, to-morrow. You don't

seem overpleased at the prospect; I'm afraid you don't appreciate poor, dear Mr. Gidley.'

'Poor, dear Mr. Gidley!' mimicked Mr. Armer. 'Why "poor dear"? you talk of him as if he were defunct.'

'Well, you know, father,' said Nellie, 'I always pity him, it must be so dreadfully lonely all by himself in that dismal great house in Bedford Square. I wonder he never married.'

'I don't think there is much material for the tender passion in Gidley's composition,' said Mr. Armer, 'he is much too devoted to certain representations of Her Majesty's head stamped on gold and silver, and the pleasing crispness of banknotes, to say nothing of deeds, mortgages, and other forms of property, which, as Mr. Bolland says on Sundays, "Time would fail me were I to endeavour to enumerate them."'

'Oh, father,' cried Nellie, 'how can you

be so hard on him? I shall always stand up for my god-father, and, indeed, father, it is not like *you* to be so bitter against anyone.'

'Well, my little mentor, I am afraid it *is* wrong of me; but, you know, Messrs. Armer and Gidley never *did* agree too well together. I think we both go better now we are in single harness. However, he is coming down, and I suppose I must make the best of it.'

'I do hope you won't quarrel as you did the last time he came to Coombridge. What a blessing it is that Jack has gone off again, for he hates Mr. Gidley too; he says, "Gidley is always sneering at him." I wonder why everybody hates the poor man so; I am sure *I* don't.'

'No, my dear,' said her father, 'I don't believe my little Nellie has it in her to hate anybody.'

'I am not so sure of that,' said Nellie, thinking of her æsthetic and irrepressible admirer; 'but *why* does everyone dislike him so? Of course I know his manners are a little—well—sarcastic . . .'

'A little!' exclaimed the squire, interrupting; 'he is the most obstinate, pig-headed . . . but, there! if I begin to discuss my valued partner's virtues, I shall lose my temper. The fact is, my dear, Mr. Gidley is one of those individuals who are never happy unless they are " in opposition," and he, consequently, is not the pleasantest of companions, and is not generally so popular as—as he might be,' concluded the squire, lamely.

'Perhaps I had better ask the rector and Mrs. Bolland to come in to dinner to-morrow?' suggested Nellie.

'I don't know,' said Mr. Armer. 'Gidley detests parsons, wants to disestablish and disendow them; it is one of his favourite topics, but he would scarcely be so rude as to "let out," as Jack says, to a clergyman's face. There is no one else you could ask on so short a notice, is there ?'

'No, not a soul,' said Nellie, 'and I think, too, that if my god-father *should* pour out the vials of his wrath against the church, Mr. Bolland is quite able to hold his own, and stand up for his cloth. Shall I send a note, then ?'

'No, you needn't trouble. I shall pass the rectory this morning, and I will look in. It will certainly be a satisfaction to me to avoid an evening's *tête-à-tête* with Gidley, and I know Bolland will come if he can.' And here the squire took up his newspaper, and the conversation dropped.

True to his word, Mr. Gidley drove up to Coombridge late in the afternoon of the next day; he came in the Coombridge dog-cart which the squire had sent to meet him. Mr. Armer was waiting in for him, and, as Mr. Gidley refused any refreshment, the two partners were soon closeted together in the library, and deep in their business. They paid no attention to the dressing-bell, and, even when that most important call, the dinner-bell, was heard, they did not seem disposed to listen to its seductive voice.

The butler waited till he could stand it no longer. he had too strong an affection for his own dinner for him to see 'the victuals a-spilin'' with equanimity, and opening the drawing-room door, where the rest of the company were assembled,

'Master give orders as he should not be disturbed, Miss Nellie,' he said, ' but hadn't I better tell him as dinner is served?'

'No, thank you, Hudson,' said Nellie. 'I think, perhaps, I had better go myself, they cannot have heard the bell ;' and, with an apology to her guests, Nellie crossed the hall to the library. As she hesitated, with her hand on the door handle, she heard the sound of voices raised considerably above their normal pitch, an unmistakable sound, indeed, of a 'very pretty quarrel.'

'You may say what you like, Gidley, but I won't be . . .' the squire was saying as his daughter opened the door; but *what* he would not be Nellie did not hear, for, hearing the door opening, he stopped short.

The squire was looking very red and ferocious; he was standing with his back against the empty fire-grate, glaring down upon Mr. Gidley, who was seated at the table, looking perfectly cool and collected, and only showing any agitation by incessantly drumming upon the leather cover with his fingers.

'What is it, Nellie?' said the squire, impatiently.

'Why, father, dinner has been waiting for ever so long; didn't you hear the bell? . . . How do you do, Mr. Gidley?' she said to that gentleman, who had arrived whilst she was out. Mr. Gidley rose and heartily greeted his god-daughter.

'Bless my soul,' said the squire, looking at his watch, 'it is a quarter to eight!
Well, it is too late for ceremony now, and
the Bollands must excuse my morning
coat. It is Mr. Gidley's fault, my dear;
he is so entertaining,' added Mr. Armer,
with a furious look at his partner, and
speaking in a sort of snarl, which sounded
very strangely to Nellie, coming, as it
came, from her usually kind and good-
humoured father.

'You are looking as fresh as a rose,
Nellie,' said Mr. Gidley, quite ignoring his
partner's ire.

'You have no time to pass compliments,
Gidley,' said the squire, who did not seem
able to regain his lost temper.

'I will just wash my hands, if you will
allow me,' answered Mr. Gidley, 'and re-
move the dust from my clothes.'

'All right, only be as quick as you can.
Here, James, show Mr. Gidley his room.'

And the two separated, to meet in a

few minutes in the drawing-room, whence they proceeded to dinner, greatly to the Reverend Walter Bolland's content, for that gentleman despised the frailties of lunch and afternoon tea, and was almost starving.

The squire was so snappish at dinner that even the satisfaction of appeasing the cravings of appetite could not prevent the rector from remarking upon such an abnormal state of affairs at Coombridge.

'The squire seems out of sorts, Nellie,' he whispered, for he had taken in the lady of the house, and sat next to her at table. 'What's the matter with him? I hope he is not ill.'

'Oh! Mr. Bolland,' whispered Nellie in return, 'I am positively trembling with fright; it is dreadful to see father so irritable. You know, he and Mr. Gidley always *do* quarrel; but I never saw father so angry with him as he is to-day. Do, please, try to keep the peace between them when Mrs. Bolland and I go into the drawing-room.'

'Now, don't you worry yourself, Nellie; *I'll* pour oil upon the troubled waters,' said the rector.

Mr. Bolland was a gentleman of an irascible temperament himself, and as Nellie looked in his face, where his notoriously bad temper was very plainly shown in an habitual frown and a dangerous glitter which occasionally appeared in his eyes, and was evident enough just then, she slightly shuddered at the very fragile reed which was all she had to lean upon. She delayed making a move as long as she could, but at last Mrs. Bolland's questioning looks (for she was longing for a chat with her favourite Nellie) and an impatient sign from her father compelled her to rise and follow the rector's wife out of the dining-room.

'My dear Nellie,' said that lady, who was fat and lymphatic, and a striking

contrast to her lean and angry spouse,
'my dear Nellie, what a time you were!
I thought you would never leave the table.
Didn't you see me nodding and looking at
you?' and she ensconced herself in a comfortable arm-chair and gave a large sigh
of content. 'What *is* the matter with
them all?' she went on. 'I couldn't get
a word out of that Mr. Gidley; your father
and he seemed to be contradicting each
other all dinner-time. It was quite awkward, my dear.'

Now Mrs. Bolland, as she frequently
remarked with much self-pity, had 'neither
chick nor child,' and she had taken the
motherless Nellie to her capacious bosom
from the very first days of the Armers'
arrival at Coombridge. Nellie responded
warmly to her affection, and there were
few thoughts or deeds of hers which were
not known to the sympathetic wife of the
rector of Coombridge.

'Father and Mr. Gidley have been shut

up together in the library for hours before dinner, and I am afraid that they have been quarrelling dreadfully. I do *wish* Mr. Gidley would not come down here, though I am always so glad to see him, for father and he are sure to fight every time he comes. I am so sorry I kept you there for so long, dear Mrs. Bolland, but I wanted them to be alone together for as short a time as possible.'

'Oh! I don't mind, dear; but I do hope that dreadful Mr. Gidley won't say anything about Radicals, or doing away with the Church, or things like that, don't you know, for I can see Walter is getting warm already at Mr. Gidley's contrariness, and, if he begins about those things, he will lose his temper with him, which would be dreadful. I'm sure I don't know sometimes *what* he gets so angry about,' said the rector's wife, with a portentous sigh.

Mrs. Bolland, after the manner of not a few stout, comfortable dames, had an extraordinary facility in muddling her pronouns, and produced ungrammatical puzzles which were intricate and confusing to the last degree, and which, sometimes, drove her impatient spouse almost frantic.

'I suppose you know, Nellie,' Mrs. Bolland went on, rambling on to another topic, 'that Lady Limborne is at the Castle?'

'Oh! yes,' answered Nellie. 'Lord Limborne was here the day before yesterday, and told us about her coming. I don't think, though, he expected his mother quite so soon.'

Mrs. Bolland took a very deep interest in the pretty little love-drama which was being played by his lordship and her favourite Nellie; for, though Nellie was too modest to make the sayings and doings and 'intentions' of possible admirers the staple of her conversation, after the custom of too many fair damsels, yet she had not succeeded in hiding from the generally obtuse Mrs. Bolland something of the 'state of affairs,' and that lady, whose husband was wont to declare that 'Grace can't see an inch beyond her nose,' and who, indeed, was constantly proclaiming as wonderful discoveries, and triumphant instances of acute penetration on her part, events which had been long known to everyone but herself, was rendered keener-eyed than usual by her interest in Nellie, and had not failed to notice several little signs on Nellie's part in regard to Lord Limborne—little rosy flushes at the approach of that favoured individual, a certain distraction in her converse when he was in sight, a turning of the face, and a slight movement of the figure towards him at the sound of his voice—such signs as these she had marked.

She had seen, moreover, that, on his part, Lord Limborne was far from averse to the society of the fair Nellie; nay, more

than once this discreet Mrs. Bolland had
earned Lord Limborne's lasting gratitude
by playing into his hands in the calmest
manner; effacing herself and most com-
placently leaving him to a *tête-à-tête* with
his adored one, engaging other folk in
conversation to the same intent, and in a
thousand ways furthering what she considered to be a most excellent match.

'For,' as she remarked to herself, in her
involved way, 'not only is he a lord, which
though Nellie may not care for it, yet *he*'
(she meant Mr. Armer) 'might, and he
hasn't too much money, with that enormous house, while *he* has heaps, and will
most certainly give a great deal to her.'

'I wonder,' she said, artfully trying to
find out 'how far things had gone,' and
settling herself comfortably in her easy-
chair—'I wonder who Lord Limborne will
marry. Do you know, my dear, I sometimes fancy he is thinking of some one of
whom I am very fond?'

As she looked Nellie straight in the face, and gave her the same smile with which she was wont to herald her wonderful 'discoveries,' it was very evident to that young lady that Mrs. Bolland had found out her secret, and the colour rose to her face and neck as the thought flashed through her mind that, if the notoriously obtuse lady at the rectory had penetrated her disguises, they must be but flimsy ones, and—horrible thought!—everyone must be talking about her and Lord Limborne. Now, though some vulgar souls may delight in the silly chaff and the 'being talked about' which not unfrequently attends the first approaches of fond lovers, yet, to a delicate mind, the very suspicion of such a thing quite destroys the sweet sense of secrecy and isolation which forms the greatest charm, to them, of these delicate tendrils and feelers in the earlier stages of this curious and composite love of ours. But Nellie did not know how affection can sharpen the very bluntest perceptions.

'I . . . I . . . am sure, I cannot tell what should make you think any such thing, dear Mrs. Bolland,' said Nellie, very red, and hesitating as she spoke.

'Well,' exclaimed her friend, cleverly changing her tack, 'I *did* think that Nellie Armer would not keep anything from her old friend; I *did* think that you would tell *me*, my dear, for I have always looked upon you almost as a daughter, and I am sure there is not a thing about me, or Walter either, for that matter, I've kept from you. I feel it very deeply, I assure you, my dear.' And the good lady was so 'worked up' by her own eloquence that she actually took out her handkerchief, and wiped two very large tears from off her ample cheeks.

Now this—of which, by the way, Mrs. Bolland *may* have had some suspicion—this was the very easiest avenue to the affectionate Nellie's heart, and she was soon

down upon her knees beside her friend,
assuring her of her great confidence in her,
and as a proof thereof, and unable also to
resist such a temptation to unburden her
mind, pouring all her hopes and fears into
Mrs. Bolland's ready ears, and with her
face hidden in that lady's lap confessing
that 'she thought Lord Limborne did . .
like her, she was sure, she did not know
why,' ('Nonsense! my love,' here interpolated her staunch admirer), 'and she . . .
she thought he was the most this, that, and
the other,' and so on, in the usual slightly
incoherent style, and greatly to Mrs.
Bolland's content; for the rector's wife,
though prosaic in person, was of a most
romantic disposition, and she positively re-
velled in this real, live love-story, so much
more interesting than the adventures, contretemps, and final bliss (in the third
volume) of the fictitious heroes and hero-
ines of the circulating library. Although
Nellie, in her new-found delight—a confi-

dante—had forgotten her fears about the un-
ruly folk in the dining-room, yet, if she had
foreseen the consequences of the angry discussion which was going on at a very high
pressure indeed in that apartment, she
would doubtless have stopped in the full
stream of her eloquence, and hastened to
pour that oil upon the troubled waters
which, in spite of his promise, the irate
rector of Coombridge certainly was *not*
pouring; on the contrary, the vials of his
wrath were unsealed, and the contents
thereof most freely discharged at the
devoted head of Mr. Gidley.

That gentleman certainly had a most
provoking manner, candid friends called it
'devilish,' and there *was* something satanic
in the calm, cold, and incisive way in which
he not only contradicted his opponent, but,
taking advantage of his hasty temper, led
him on to take up positions he could not
defend, and, with the utmost politeness,
accompanied by a pitying sneer, proved

him to be in the wrong. All was grist that came to Mr. Gidley's mill: he contradicted everything; he was angry with Mr. Armer; they had had a more than usually warm business encounter that afternoon, and Armer's obstinacy had been too firm for his partner for once. Mr. Gidley saw he must return to town without having gained the object of his visit. Always more or less 'contrairy,' (as nurses say of some children), he was wrought up to a white heat of rage, and was, consequently, more insultingly urbane than ever. The roads, gastronomy, wines, the last new book, each and everything furnished him with an opportunity of relieving his rage at the expense of the devoted rector (for the squire maintained a sulky silence), who, as the aggressive one usually himself, could hardly contain himself in the position in which, it must be owned, he had very often placed other people. At last Mr. Gidley remarked that ' he could not imagine how people employed

their time in such retired villages as Coombridge, how they avoided the almost inevitable stagnation which must attend upon
an idle, desultory life.'

'What do you mean by idle; for I suppose you refer to me?' said the rector,
with some warmth; for Mr. Gidley's remarks were addressed to him.

'Why, my dear sir,' returned Mr. Gidley, 'pardon me, I did not mean anything
personal. I was merely speaking generally. But, since you invite the question,
I *should* like to know how you employ
your time. I have often wondered what
on earth the country clergy do with themselves; for, of course, it is absurd to suppose that the limited population of their
parishes can employ them constantly in
visiting the sick and performing the
offices of the church. I suppose, now,
you do a good deal in your garden?' he
went on, with a sort of patronising tone,
eminently irritating. 'Grow—ah—cab-

bages, or go in for rose-growing, and
that sort of thing, eh? Gossip with the
farmers; and—upon my word, I *should*
like to know what you do with your time.'

'Sir,' said Mr. Bolland, who had been
listening to this exordium with great im-
patience and wrath. 'Sir,' he said, rising
from his seat, 'your insulting remarks cast
a slur upon a class of men who have
higher thoughts and aspirations than I
could explain to a man of your, unfortunately, low tone of mind, and who have——'

'My *dear* sir,' interrupted his antagonist,
'I assure you I had not the least intention
of insulting you, or "casting a slur" upon
any class of men; and you must allow me
to remark, in my turn, that it ill beseems
a man of your sacred calling to insult an
inoffensive individual by supposing the
tone of his mind to be "low." My *dear*
sir—*low*, I beg of you—*low!*'

It was not so much the words—which
were, indeed, in themselves nothing so

very provoking—it was the nasty, sneering tone of the man's voice, and his evident amusement at the rector's expense, which roused that individual to a pitch of ire he found to be insupportable: an almost irrepressible desire to hurl the nearest decanter at the placid Gidley's head possessed his soul, and, to avoid such an unseemly display on his part, he begged his host's permission to retire, and, with a withering look at his adversary, he withdrew from the contest, and joined his wife and Nellie in the drawing-room.

Now, the squire had refused to be drawn into the wordy fight, which had raged with more or less of rancour between his partner and Mr. Bolland ever since the ladies had withdrawn their restraining presence. He seemed depressed, or, to put it plainly, Mr. Armer was sulking, and, whilst indulging in this unromantic attitude of mind, he (a most abstemious man as a rule) filled up his glass almost unconsciously; and, in short, drank a great deal more wine than was his wont, or was good for him.

As soon, then, as the door banged upon the exit of the irate rector, and he realised that his friend and guest had been galled beyond endurance by his partner's abominable, sneering rudeness, he suddenly roused himself from his morose fit, and, losing all control over himself, he poured out such a volume of vituperation upon Mr. Gidley as effectually silenced that gentleman. This is a kind of eloquence which grows with its exercise, particularly, as in the squire's case, when stimulated by copious draughts of wine; and as the accumulated anger of years at length had its vent, and old grievances were dragged to light, and the injuries of the present were urged in language which, if not choice, was certainly forcible enough, as the squire gathered from every source, and overwhelmed his partner with a very deluge of wrath,

Mr. Gidley for once lost *his* composure, and, turning absolutely white and trembling with rage, he cried out,

'Enough! enough, sir! you—you poor fool! I have borne with your besotted obstinacy long enough, I can do without your money now, and you shall go to the devil your own way, for I will never speak to you again!' And, with that, his trembling hands opened the door, and he passed out, and, going straight to his bed-room, he packed again the hand-bag which contained all that he had brought with him, and, leaving the house without any farewells whatever, he marched to the village inn (greatly to the astonishment of the bibulous cronies there assembled), and, rising early after a most uncomfortable night spent in that homely hostelry, he drove in to catch the first train to town from Exeter, determined never to set foot in Coombridge again.

His burst of anger come thus to a sudden end by the retreat of its object, and the squire thus left alone, the consequences—those exceedingly unpleasant intruders—began slowly to dawn upon his faculties with a most sobering effect. One of the advantages of his partnership with Gidley was his absolute and entire confidence in his partner's honesty, clearheadedness, and caution; Gidley's had always been the guiding hand from the very first, and it was this guiding at which the senior partner (in name, if in nothing else) of the firm displayed opposition, although he knew well enough the value of Gidley's restraining influence, and had seen in many instances what disasters would have followed had he been suffered to have his own way.

Mr. Armer had by far the larger amount of capital, and it galled him beyond measure to see how, notwithstanding this fact, he had to 'play second fiddle,' and how very well it was for him that he *did* so

often have to perform upon that obnoxious
instrument. It was this confidence in his
partner which, together with the irksome-
ness of so often having to give way, led
him to give up at last, and almost entirely,
any active share in the business, to con-
fide his capital to Mr. Gidley's care with
but little overlooking, and to follow out a
long-cherished idea, and settle down as a
country magnate.

Now, if Mr. Gidley meant what he had
just said—and the squire owned to himself that Mr. Gidley usually *did* mean
what he said, and had, moreover, a very
thorough way of carrying out that meaning—if Gidley stuck to his threat, and refused to have anything more to do with
his partner, this would mean very many
unpleasant consequences *to* that partner.
It would mean that he must manipulate
his own capital, and either reduce his ex-
penses considerably (for the cautious and
knowing Gidley secured by his transactions

a high interest for the firm's money), or
he must go back himself to his old haunts,
and seek by clever financial operations—
and speculation had always been a temptation to him—to realise such a sum of
money as should establish him firmly in
his present way of living, and at the same
time give him the laugh over the slow and
careful Gidley.

'"Go to the devil your own way"?
Ah,' said the squire to himself, 'I have
not so long left the City as to have lost
touch; I think I know something of
financing still, and I will show Master
Gidley that I can get along well enough—
ay, and a great deal better, too—without
his help than with it.'

Now, although Mr. Armer had virtually
given up the reins into Mr. Gidley's hands,
yet he was, of course, kept informed as
to the larger transactions of the firm of
Armer and Gidley, and he had at all times
gained a great deal of pleasure from watch-

ing the fluctuations of the money-market, dotting down different enterprises, or rather speculations, he would have indulged in himself, had it not been for the restraining hand of his partner; and, as he sat there alone, the squire almost forgot his rage, and his apprehensions as to the consequences thereof, in the happy thought that now he could, without any gainsaying, display that acuteness and prophetic foresight of his which, he felt, were lights too long hidden. Visions of successful ' coups,' which might have been made if his advice had been taken, rose to his memory; for, of course, he quite lost sight of the dozens of times when Mr. Gidley's veto had put a stopper on ventures which must have brought about disastrous fiascoes. No, he forgot all the failures, and remembered only the wonderful successes which would certainly have rewarded *some* of these ventures of his.

'With **my** experience,' he thought to

himself, 'and with my foresight I ought to
made a perfectly colossal fortune ; with
my capital to operate with, I ought to
have thousands where I now have hundreds.'

He had long ceased to care about
accumulating money, for years he had
been contented with his already ample
fortune : but the desire to show to the
provokingly cautious Gidley that he was
not such a fool as he took him for, the
itch for the old excitement, and the opportunity Gidley's threat opened up of
getting his capital to himself, and of indulging himself in his long-suppressed
desire for the perilous game of speculation, woke up slumbering acquisitiveness,
and Mr. Armer then and there made up
his mind to take his partner at his word,
and to begin to pile up a huge fortune
upon the substantial foundation which he
already possessed. Smiling at these golden
visions, the squire rose from his chair, and

went to the drawing-room, where he found
the worthy rector alone, still looking very
angry, and waiting for his wife's appearance; for she was going through the long
and tedious (to her husband, at least)
operation of 'putting on her things,' and
was assisted in that ceremony by the
affectionate Nellie.

'How you can put up with that man
Gidley is more than I can understand,
Armer,' said Mr. Bolland. 'I never met
with such impertinence in my life—it's—
it's abominable, sir!' and the angry little
man actually spluttered with rage.

'I am sorry, Bolland, he should have
annoyed you in that way, but I don't think
he will do so again. I've spoken plainly
to him' (he had indeed), 'and I don't
think we shall . . . hush-sh-sh,' said the
squire, as the voices of Mrs. Bolland and
Nellie made them to be heard, 'hush! don't
say anything to my daughter; you *haven't*
said anything, eh?'

'No, no,' whispered the rector, 'they were not here when I came out of the dining-room.——Well, my dear,' he said to his wife, when she appeared, 'I hope you are satisfied with the beauty of your toilette, you have been long enough about it, anyhow; I have been waiting here for more than half-an-hour.'

'Oh, it was *my* fault,' said Nellie, 'I kept Mrs. Bolland talking.'

'Well, I know she loves a "tell," as Devonshire folks say, with you; and so do I, for that matter. Now, Mrs. Bolland! Good-night, squire; good-night, Nellie.'

And, tucking his stout spouse's arm under his own, the active little rector trotted off with his large, and, in a very short time, breathless better half.

CHAPTER VII.

THE TEIGNBRIDGE 'LADIES' DAY.'

JAMES, Lord Limborne, of Limborne Castle, in the county of Devon, was not having a particularly good time of it in his baronial halls, for, although his mother imagined she was far too well-bred to descend to wranglings and bickerings, she had a very good idea of the various other ways of making herself disagreeable notwithstanding, and she took every opportunity of showing her son how deeply disappointed she felt at what she called his want of common sense, and his foolishness in not taking immediate advantage of the result of her matrimonial manœuvres.

She had, indeed, taken infinite pains to gain her end in regard to the Lady Emily, and her position in the delicate negotiation had greatly jarred against her haughty and reticent nature: to hint and sound, to make cautious advances with the chance of a more or less decided rebuff, to go through all the pretty little diplomacies of a kind of suitor—all this was gall and wormwood to Lady Limborne; but her success repaid her for all; and as, her embassy over, she was travelling down to Devonshire, she acknowledged that the result infinitely overbalanced the dis-comfort of the struggle, and, exulting at the pleasant picture of which all this most repugnant work was the end, she passed some very pleasant hours in the railway carriage in imagining all these happy consequences.

Her dear James married to one of the greatest prizes in the matrimonial market (although this was far from *her* way of

expressing it), James married to Emily
Beldon, *lié* with the great political House
of Beldon, a rich peer, young, clever, energetic, and ambitious—there was no limit to
the horizon which stretched out before the
happy couple. James in the Cabinet, his wife
a leader of 'ton,' and the Dowager Lady
Limborne basking in the refulgent light of
all this magnificence! The old Castle
once more restored to its ancient lordly
splendour, the dilapidated furniture, the
dismal unkemptness of the grounds, the
venerable and racketty carriage, the poor
and inefficient service—all these sharp
stings to her pride and consequence things
of the past, and the Limborne family once
again lifting up its head boldly among the
best of all the land.

Such thoughts as these had occupied her
pleasantly, effaced the tedium of the hot
and dusty journey, and given an added
delight to her pleasure in seeing her son—
the centre figure of her mind-picture—

again. The fall from such a height was far from pleasant; the shabbiness of her surroundings never before seemed so hateful and hopeless, and, although she did not by any means intend to 'throw up the cards,' yet, for the moment, the shock had been almost more than Lady Limborne could bear, and she was, therefore, cold and distant, and, if one might use such an expression of so exalted a personage, downright disagreeable to her son.

Of course, Lord Limborne knew well enough the depth of his mother's disappointment. He was profoundly sorry for her, for he loved her dearly ; this so evident change in her manner was a constant source of pain to him, and he trembled to think of her bitter anger when he should have to tell her—as tell her he must, if he should be successful with Nellie—of his attachment to that young lady. Gladly then did he hail any distraction which should take his mother and himself 'out of themselves' even for a single day, and he looked forward to the approaching 'Ladies' Day' at the Teignbridge Club with quite a school-boy eagerness, for not only would it bring a relief from the 'strained relations' of his every-day life, but also the certain delight of again seeing the girl who was occupying more and more of his thoughts, throwing his money troubles even into the background, and playing havoc with his literary work.

Now, not to know all about Teignbridge shows men and women to be altogether outside the pale of society in South Devon; and many heads a great deal fairer, if, perhaps, not so well furnished as Lord Limborne's were occupied with thoughts of the momentous Thursday. Dear to the feminine heart is the prospect of displaying to an envious and cavilling, or possibly an admiring, world, a gorgeous, startling, or piquante costume; and dear, too, it must be confessed, to the male heart is a mild indulgence in personal vanity (in this matter, indeed, there is but little to choose between the sexes, and the tailor has as much to answer for as the milliner). Now the 'Ladies' Day' at Teignbridge affords an excellent opportunity for indulgence in these amiable vices of personal pride and vanity; here morning costume is *de rigueur*, and fancy is allowed to run the utmost riot in the shape and colour of gowns, hats, or bonnets, and all the other etceteras of the beloved and cherished toilette.

A long, low, thatched house, a green-bowered verandah, smooth and well-kept lawns, a soft and balmy summer evening, groups of well-clad gentlefolks, the babbling of much talk, now and again a silvery laugh, much gossiping of dowagers under the verandah, more flirting between fair demoiselles and preux-chevaliers in quiet nooks—all this, and much more *with-*

out; and *within*, a large expanse of smooth floor, 'giving' slightly (as all floors meant to be danced upon should ' give '), sufficient light, an excellent band, and alas ! too many gyrating couples—such is Teignbridge on the ' Ladies' Days.'

As Lady Limborne and her son arrived, after a long and somewhat awkward *tête-à-tête* drive through the lovely and execrably-kept roads and lanes of this part of Devonshire, the early dinner, which precedes the dance on these occasions, was some time over; the room was cleared of its impedimenta ; the balmy odours of the ' cold collection ' had vanished, and the dancing was already in full swing; the band were scraping and blowing to melodious purpose at one of Waldteufel's entrancing waltzes, and the various degrees of dancers were enjoying the bliss of the past-masters in the art, or enduring the agonies of the tyro. It was, as a hunting parson remarked (for this genus is not yet extinct in fair Devonia), 'a full meet,' and Lord Limborne and his mother were soon exchanging greetings with many friends.

Leaving Lady Limborne seated comfortably, and descanting to a congenial companion on the glories of past 'Teignbridges,' and the pale reflection of those glories which the present festivity afforded, our lover, Lord Limborne, was soon gently strolling around, eagerly searching for the idol of his heart—the fair and piquante Nellie.

'There seems to be a strange set of people here,' said Lady Limborne to her companion, lifting the while a pair of pince-nez to her eyes and surveying the moving throng. 'What a number of vulgar-looking men and women; that small and stout man with the tall wife —I suppose—and loudly-dressed daughters: how can such people as they are possibly gain an entrance here?'

'Don't you know them?' said her friend, an old, long-retired admiral of high descent, redolent of club-land rather than of the briny ocean. 'They are neighbours of yours. That stout little man is the new millionaire, the man who has bought Wreford—don't you know? They are immensely rich, and, I hear, frightfully vulgar—the man drops his "h's," and that kind of thing; the girls are not bad-looking, if some one would only teach them how to dress. *One* of them is positively handsome.'

'Of course I have heard that some City people had bought Wreford, and were spending large sums of money there. So *those* are the people!' said Lady Limborne, looking at our friends the Dentons rather intently. 'I suppose they are impossible? One could not know them?'

'In these days, my dear Lady Limborne,' said the old gentleman, shrugging his shoulders, '*nothing* is impossible. A fellow got into our club the other day, proposed by a peer of the realm, and seconded by a baronet—a fellow who made his money in skins! Fact, I assure you —skins!' and he ruminated sadly on the unsavoury origin of his club-fellow's fortune. 'After *that*,' he went on, 'you can expect almost anything. Shouldn't wonder if we had soap or tallow next. I don't know where these Dentons got *their* money; butchers make enormous fortunes now-a-days, and *he* looks like a butcher, don't you think? There is a kind of *shining* look about him that I have noticed in butchers . . . positively!' he exclaimed, in a tone of great alarm, 'they are coming here! I . . . I . . . think . . .'

But *what* he thought must be lost to posterity, as it was to Lady Limborne, for Mr. and Mrs. Denton, convoyed by a voluminous and jovial-looking dame, were rapidly bearing down upon that particular point of vantage where Lady Limborne and her friend were seated.

'How d'ye do, Lady Limborne?' said
the voluminous one, in a loud and genial
tone. 'Let me introduce you to your
neighbours—for Wreford is the next place
to Limborne, you know—Mr. and Mrs.
Denton.'

Nobody (as Lady Limborne afterwards
remarked), nobody but Charlotte Ingle
would have had the effrontery and bad
taste to introduce people so widely separated, so utterly unlikely to 'mix,' as the
proud chatelaine of Limborne and the inhabitants of Wreford. But, indeed, that
rotund and jovial spinster was capable of
even worse social sins than this one. Entirely devoid of that useful quality—tact,
thoroughly satisfied with herself, and perfectly persuaded that everyone was cap-
tivated by her gay insouciance and
debonnaire joviality, she absolutely *forced*
herself into intimacies which her really
good birth and multitudinous connections
in the county made it extremely difficult,

though eminently desirable, to avoid; unable to see that she was in *any* way
objected to, she *would* be confidential,
bantering, loudly applauding, or as loudly
condemning. Folks watched her approach
with something of the trembling of the
bird at the coming of the cat (though
there was nothing of the silence and the
slyness of feline attack in Miss Ingle's
onslaughts), it was impossible to escape;
she had a voice, a loud and piercing voice,
and could use it, on occasion, in a manner
which would, in the most painful way, call
the attention of all bystanders to the
individual thus arrested in a futile attempt
to slip away unaccosted.

All sorts and conditions of men and
women were alike the objects of her attention and regard; she was perfectly un-
trammeled by any social niceties, and mere
curiosity (of which vice she possessed no
inconsiderable stock) was quite enough to
make her seek, and very soon, and against

all obstacles, find some excuse for acquaintanceship. Some rumours of the magnificence of Wreford, and of the fabulous wealth of the owner thereof, had reached her, and it was not long before she had found a friend who moved in the Wreford orbit, had obtained an introduction, and had formed one of her sudden, violent intimacies with the family: Mr. Denton's vulgarity amused her, she liked Mrs. Denton and the girls, and found a consummate joy in treading upon the corns of the æsthetic Henry. So friendly was she that an invitation to stay at Wreford quickly followed upon her introduction to the family, and the customary interchange of visits.

Miss Ingle, who loved the good things of this life, was charmed with the comfortable magnificence which the great upholsterer to whom the internal furnishing of the mansion was committed had displayed, and she rejoiced in the daily-recurring

allurements of the French *chef* who presided over the culinary department; in
fact, she 'took up' (as she called it) the
Dentons, and determined, still in her
choice language, to 'run them in society.'
Hence her appearing with them at Teignbridge, for which somewhat exclusive entertainment she had procured them, by
importunate begging, the necessary tickets,
and hence her introduction of the round
and rubicund Mr. Denton, and his tall and
not inelegant spouse, to Lady Limborne,
and to many other willing and unwilling
acquaintances.

Schooled by his wife, the amiable master
of Wreford restricted his conversation, on
this his first introduction to what he called
'the tip-toppers,' to the ordinary amenities of such early stages of acquaintanceship, somewhat accentuated, on his part,
by determined and hearty hand-shakings;
though his wife had that very morning
begged him to abstain from such undue

familiarities with the ladies to whom he should be presented.

'I can't help it,' he had said, when his better-half rebuked him on their return; 'my 'and seems to come out like one of them automatums as I used to see at the old Colisseum, and, for the life of me, when it's out I don't know what to do with it *but* shake 'ands;' and shake hands he did, and with extraordinary vigour.

This, and certain other small wanderings from the ordinary customs of 'the world,' together with a *malaise* which not one of the family could *quite* shake off on this their first appearance, disposed people to look with a cold eye upon these new claimants to social intercourse in South Devon. But great is Gold now-a-days, and mightily does it prevail. The old admiral was wise in his generation, and, though Lady Limborne was as cold as her fear of the fair Charlotte Ingle would permit her to be to these debutants, yet

a whisper of the immense wealth which
Australia had poured into Uncle Ben's
lap, and thence into the Wreford coffers,
quickly altered the complexion of affairs,
turned Mr. Denton's vulgarity into 'so
eccentric, don't you know!' Miss Denton's
'gush' into 'such an unaffected girl; no
nonsense about *her!*' and changed the
young man's absurd, hang-dog ways into
quite a Byronic melancholy; so that the
day ended most auspiciously for Mrs. Denton's proud hopes of 'society'; and, though
Mr. Denton wondered why that Lady Limborne of whom they were always talking
was 'so 'igh and 'aughty,' and 'what she
gave herself sich airs for,' his wife, his
son, and his two fair daughters rejoiced
in their triumph, and dreamed all the way
home of coronets, weddings in high life,
columns in the fashionable newspapers,
and all the other 'agremens' in which the
vulgar rich live and move and have their
loftiest being.

The cup, however, of the devoted Henry's joy was not without an exceeding bitter flavour, for, search as he would, or could rather (for his father clung to him with a desperate persistence in this embarrassing 'first appearance'), gaze about as he did, he failed to discover the lovely Nellie, and deep was his disgust at having to leave without seeing his beloved. Some conversation with the 'beloved object's' brother he *did* have, however, but this by no means consoled him; for Master Jack Armer seized upon this opportunity with greediness, and getting Henry Denton into a quiet corner, whilst Denton *père* was solacing himself at the refreshment bar, he satisfied a long-felt craving, and gave Henry 'a bit of his mind' about Henry's conduct at Cambridge and elsewhere, which annoyed that obtuse individual very much, but did not in the least deter him from going on in his hopeless quest; for Nellie's estimate of the general flabbiness of his character was a right one —and, punch him as hardly as you would, he quickly returned to his old condition, and the punishment left no mark.

CHAPTER VIII.

LORD LIMBORNE PROPOSES.

WHERE *was* Nellie, then, that, carefully as he sought her, Henry Denton failed to find her? There is—or it may be *was*, for things small as well as great change in this fickle world of ours—a certain little tent which, during the cricket-match that preceded the Teignbridge dinner and dance held the person who scored the various runs, byes, and wides which but feebly kept the attention of the few early arrivals of the gentler sex, who, in sooth, were longing for the evening, and gave pleasant excitement, and at the same time appetite for the cold collation and the sherry to the *habitués* of the male persuasion.

Now, this tent served a double purpose :
the scorer's tent by day, by *night* it not
infrequently exchanged the varying fortunes of the cricket-match **for** the monotonous but ever entrancing (to the persons
concerned) story of the loves of the mortals.
Many kinds **of** lovers have sought its
friendly shelter, from those **who** were, with
hesitating speech, making the first timid
advances, **on** through the various degrees,
the first slight hand-pressure, the rosy
blush at **a very** well-intentioned but most
probably somewhat broad compliment (for
this art of delicate compliment is rare indeed) the offer and acceptance, or the
hesitating request, for that universal **coin**
of love, **a** flower, and so on **to** the fully
assured bliss **of** those whose mutual affections are approved by parents and **an ap-**
plauding world, and who (the *male* birds, we
should premise) **already find** that sweets
have a habit **of cloying, and** who do most
sincerely incline **to a** cigar which ' a fellow

can smoke in peace and quiet, don't you know,' and not in the spasmodic manner rendered necessary by the exigencies of pre-connubial bliss.

Now, if there was one place in the world which Lord Limborne would have avoided as the scene of the avowal of his passion, that place was Teignbridge; and of all the corners, verandahs, tents, lawns, rooms, and so forth which together make up this gathering place of the South Devon clans, the particular tent in question was the one spot which his soul would have loathed to look upon as the witness of his fervid outpourings of love. But, alas for the irony of Fate! here was his good-humouredly cynical, superior, and learned lordship in this very identical tent, seated in extremely close proximity to his goddess, in a most lack-adaisical, not to say loving attitude, to wit with his arm (forgive me, ye prudish ones!) his arm, I say, around the fair Nellie's waist, and himself talking as arrant non-

sense as ever enamoured swain poured
into the ready ears of 'Amaryllis in the
shade;' and I would not give the proverbial ' tuppence ' for any man ' as calls himself a man ' (as the Seven Dials' ladies remark) who has not been in precisely the
same attitude, and with the very same
feelings, with *his* Dulcinea, whether she be
yet young, and sweet as a dewy rose, or
now fat, fair, and forty, and the mother of
many, or the venerable partner of his
declining years as he and she toddle on
together adown the vale of life.

Verily, it was with Lord Limborne as with
most other love-sick swains, the climax of
his love-story was sudden and unexpected;
and very different in its scene, and its re-
lation, was this crowning chapter of the
volume, in which the two fond souls for
the first time confessed their mutual flame
and solaced themselves after the universal
manner of all lovers, whether they be the
Chloes and Lubins of the rustic lanes, the

toilworn lads and lasses of the factory towns, or of those high-born and wealthy ones whose love-affairs are trumpeted forth in noble style in the columns of the society papers.

Something of romance, it is felt by us all, should mark this first outburst of long-pent-up feelings, something of poesy there should be in the surroundings; the silence of a sun-flecked, shady avenue in some summer wood, the stillness of night, and the mystery of moonlight on some such balcony as heard the loves of Romeo and Juliet; some murmuring of the sea, perhaps, as we wander together, with many a halt, by the soft-sounding marge : ay ! and as the fragrant smoke of our sacrifice to St. Nicotiana (for, heaven forbid that I, a poor male unit, should dare to peer into the hidden penetralia of feminine love-reverie !) as the smoke of our cigar vanishes and comes again in graceful wreaths, the very *words* of our avowal come readily to the mind, and we silently apostrophise the 'divine She,' in a fervid flow of rhapsody, such as *must*, we fondly imagine, bear her away in its resistless tide, and give us a victory over any signs of hesitancy we may have marked in our more despondent moods.

But the reality! how widely different from these fond dreams! Where is that eloquence which seemed *natural* to us, and the occasion in our solitary musings? Where is the 'fervid flow' afore-mentioned in the presence of the beloved one? What? This stuttering, halting individual, this person of the purple face, the ungraceful action, the silly speech—this the hero of the fateful hour? the persuasive softener of difficulties? the eloquent inspirer of love? the utterer of impassioned, burning periods? Ah! many a poor fellow has cut a ridiculous figure enough at such a supreme moment, and good, honest heart has spoken, if haltingly, yet most sincerely, if without much eloquence, yet with earnestness enough, God wot! And heaven's blessings on that inborn wit of woman, which allows her to see, in that often pitiful figure at her feet, a romance enough for her, and the very lover she desires above all the other flutterers around the shining light.

Not the least idea of putting his fortune to the touch, and declaring his passion to Nellie, had Lord Limborne on that sunny Thursday as he looked here and there for her sweet face in the throng of dark and fair, young and old, plain and lovely (for, in sooth, the Devonshire maidens have a pleasing habit of loveliness). No conjuncture of events could have been more inauspicious for such an avowal; a very gradual process must be the letting down of Lady Limborne from the heights of the Beldon alliance to the lower (albeit pleasanter) valley of this Coombridge project, and all bold plunges, all sudden sur-

prises must be avoided in the present state
of 'strained relations.'

Thinking, however, of the more immediate future, and letting the remoter
possibilities take care of themselves, wondering how Nellie would look when he
should happen upon her, whether he should
be able, with love's cunning, (how often a
mistaken cunning, a *too* sharp seeing where
naught was to be seen, let those who have
made the mistake, and met with the consequent rebuff, tell!) whether he should be
able to catch some fleeting sign of expec-
tation, interest, or dawning love, a slight
wild-rose flush perhaps, some little tremu-
lous motion of the hand. Thinking such
thoughts as these, Lord Limborne very
soon perceived the fairy-like form of Helen
Armer, attended by Jack, her vivacious
brother. Lord Limborne was soon by
Nellie's side, and by 'a fortuitous com-
bination of circumstances,' (as the young
curate expressed it, after he was rebuked

by his rector for using the words 'a lucky chance' in the pulpit), by Fortune's favour, and not, to say the truth, without the connivance of the obstructing party—who had, indeed, his own amusement to provide for—rid of the gallant Jack, Lord Limborne found himself in the position he most desired, to wit, alone with the lovely Nellie.

It is true report said there were several hundreds of one sex or the other at Teignbridge that day, but they were of no account with the enamoured ones, who quickly, by mutual consent, and almost unconsciously, sought the more perfect solitude which the far end of the smooth-shaven lawn afforded. Here, in pleasant converse, to and fro they wandered; until some imp of night, fluttering hither and thither on busy mischief intent, whispered to Lord Limborne that Nellie must be tired, conducted them, unconscious of harm, to that seductive tent, left them in the close contiguity which the narrowness of that temple of Cupid rendered necessary, and flew off to do some other Puckish trick upon some other unsuspecting persons.

Now the seat (which replaced the scorer's chair) was not *very* much too large for one fairly bulky person, and was certainly scarcely large enough for two, even though one of the two should be the slim and light-built Nellie; hence, when the adoring James seated himself beside the fair object of his adoration—which he very presently *did*—personal contact became unavoidable without an expenditure of 'scrooging,' which the occasion and the persons present scarcely demanded; hence, too, a certain nervousness which the fair Helen felt at this unaccustomed proximity communicated itself, as nervousness is wont, to the other individual, and a silence followed which was felt on both sides to be particularly awkward. It was, perhaps, to break this awkwardness that Lord Lim-

borne gently possessed himself of Nellie's
hand, and it was because she was so nervous, probably, that she failed to withdraw
it, as she most certainly ought to have
done.

But why our 'potent, grave,' if not
'reverent' signor should have suddenly
blurted out a stammering confession of
love, I cannot tell, unless it was the
touch of that soft, warm, white hand;
the love that was in him, that unconscionable little imp again, or, perhaps,
Cupid himself, the deity of the bower.
So it was, however, and so it was, too,
that this beauteous Helen confessed, with
downcast eyes and the sweetest blush in
the world, that she *did*—well, I will spare
the reader both the lover's rhapsodies and
the maid's shy responses thereto, persuaded of the gratitude of the mass of
my readers, though, here and there, some
sentimental miss may wish it had been
otherwise.

There is, as painful experience teaches us all sooner or later, a seamy side to most of the various garments which go to make up this life-attire of ours, and it is a truism to say that love's young dream has too often a harsh enough awakening. Poor, happy souls! let them rejoice together for a few brief moments over this glorious secret they have just brought to light, forgetting that there are such things in the world as stern parents (of either sex), the grinding poverty of the 'shabby-genteel,' a somewhat absurd family pride, and other little barriers which must be surmounted before Hymen's altar shall be crowned with flowers, the sacred rite performed, and the happy couple departed to the 'residence of Lord Some-one or other,' in a shower of rice, and slippers, and blessings.

A simple and very natural remark, on Nellie's part, quickly put to rout her lover's ecstatic thoughts, and introduced elements of disturbance even in this very early stage of their joint love-affair.

'How pleased father will be,' she murmured. 'He always liked you so much, and he often speaks of you. Do you know, I sometimes think he must have some suspicion of all this, though why I cannot imagine.'

Mr. Armer must, indeed, have been a very blind individual not to have seen, and possessed of a great deal more dulness than he would have cared to own, not to have speculated upon the evident attentions bestowed by his noble neighbour upon his only daughter; and this probability made the whole affair still more involved and hopeless.

If there was one vice Lord Limborne detested more than the others, that vice was insincerity. Steadfast as a rock in his opinions, and sufficiently courageous in proclaiming them, he despised anything that savoured of deceit or double-dealing;

and yet here, in the most important crisis
of his life, he found himself doing (as how
many of us find *our*selves doing) the very
thing he had often loudly condemned in
others, and initiating his *fiancée* into ways
of concealment and consequent deceit.

'Nellie dear,' he said, after wondering
how he should put so delicate a matter
to her, ' you know my mother is the dearest mother in the world' (here Nellie, who
was a shrewd little lassie, began to look
for the inevitable 'but' which follows
upon such superlatives), 'and she loves me
very dearly. I verily believe she would cut
off her right hand for me; you see, I am
her only child, and she has no one else in
the world to think of; so you must not
mind her exalted ideas of me.'

All this time Nellie was waiting and wondering what *could* be the upshot of this
lengthy exordium.

'Well,' Lord Limborne went on, floun-
dering about in a wordy bog, and not see-

ing his way out of it, 'well, you know, she thinks me a kind of Admirable Crichton, a—a genius, and that I only want time and opportunity to develop into something quite of the most remarkable . . . I don't know why I am talking in this idiotic way, and no wonder you look so surprised, darling; but don't be angry with me, I could not bear that.'

'I am not likely to be angry with you,' said Nellie, not liking to call her lover 'James' as yet, and deeming Lord Limborne too formal, and therefore leaving out names altogether; 'but what is it? Why should you talk of Lady Limborne as if you were making excuses?'

'Well, the truth is,' said Lord Limborne, determined to rid himself of the unpleasant facts at one fell swoop, 'the truth is, my mother has been trying to "arrange" (I believe that is the correct term) to arrange a marriage between your humble servant and a very exalted damsel indeed.

Now wait a minute, Nellie !' he hurriedly
exclaimed, as some premonitory wrigglings
warned him of a disposition on Nellie's
part to ' sever the connection ;' ' let me tell
you all, and then I will abide by all you
say ; only remember that my mother knows
nothing of *this* ' (she would have been extremely shocked if she had come suddenly
upon what Lord Limborne was pleased to
call ' this ') ; ' she knows, of course, that I
am often at Coombridge, but she thinks it
is more to see your father and Jack ; and,
—in fact, it is no use beating about, I
must tell you—she is very obstinate, and
deeply set in any plans of hers. She has,
in a kind of way, and without consulting
me, committed herself to these Beldous,
and I intended to wait, and not to have
spoken to you, until all these matters had
settled themselves : but you know, Nellie,
you looked so lovely and I felt so——'
and here followed another rhapsody, and
accompaniments thereto.

'Well, but what does it all mean? What do you want me to do?' were Nellie's not unnatural questions, on emerging from the afore-mentioned accompaniment. 'Do you want me to release you from the engagement?' she added, with a wicked little smile.

'No; but, Nellie, I am afraid we had better not speak to anyone about it for a little while,' said Lord Limborne, too anxious to be jesting. 'I *hate* asking you to do such a thing for me—indeed, I hate all mysteries and concealments—but if you care for me, as I know now you do care, you will bear this. My mother and I are on very uncomfortable terms at this very time, most unfortunately, and about this abominable marriage plan of hers too. I never remember a single cloud between us before.'

Now Nellie knew very well indeed that, if Lady Limborne was proud, Squire Armer was proud too, and that if Lady Limborne shewed any sign of dislike to her (Nellie's) engagement to James, the very fact of the Limbornes' rank would be a spur (if, indeed, any spur save opposition on *any* score were wanted) to goad her father to the most determined resistance, and she knew his obstinacy well enough to be able to predict that not even his beloved Nellie's grief would suffice to gain his consent to his daughter's entering a family where her marriage was likely to be looked upon as a *mésalliance.*

Nor was Nellie sure herself whether her affection for Lord Limborne would be strong enough to conquer *her* pride. Still, she had learnt to love Lady Limborne's son, and she had just heard that Lord Limborne loved her, Nellie Armer, and if a little time could smooth over these unexpected difficulties, which, after all, did not appear to her to be so very insurmountable (she did not know her ladyship) —and she was very much in love, and the adoring James was looking at her very beseechingly, and altogether it was too much for the fair Helen, so that before they glided into the throng, with such nonchalant air as they were able to assume, matters were arranged between them, and no one was to be told the great news—at any rate, for that indefinite period, 'a little while.'

CHAPTER IX.

A MOVE TO HAMPSTEAD.

'MASTER were terrible put about, sure enough,' said Charles, the youthful footman, who, with the portly Hudson, represented the male element in the Coombridge indoors *ménage*. Now Charles was of Devonshire 'extraction.' 'Terrible put about he were,' he went on ; 'I never see un so took aback, her went off this morning like thunder.'

'Such a pleasant-spoken gentleman as squire is, too,' said Mary Housemaid, 'so haffable.'

'Well,' said Charles, 'I seem there's sommut wrong, for he wouldn't hardly say nothun to Miss Nellie, and as for young Mas'r Jack, why, her never so much as gave un the "good-bye."'

'Put about' our good squire was, truly, for he had had two very unpleasant epistles by that morning's post, one from partner Gidley, in which the said Gidley desired the squire to take his capital to himself, and at the same time gently hinted at the need of caution in manipulating that capital, in his own peculiar sneering way, and greatly to Mr. Armer's rage and indignation. Mr. Gidley also declined to see his partner, and desired that any communications he might deem it necessary to make should be made through his solicitors. Now this was of itself quite enough to inflame Mr. Armer's ire, and he was already at 'blood heat' when he opened the second letter. This informed him of liabilities the extravagant Jack had formed at Cambridge, and sent him at once to 'boiling point,' and produced an explosion at the breakfast-table which quickly drove

Nellie from the **room, and left the defence-less Jack** exposed **to the full force** of the volcanic eruption.

Well might **the squire rage and fume,** for the considerable sum **of** money Jack **had named** as the total of his **debts on** 'going down' was very far short indeed of that unconscionable total itself, and his father freely accused his son **of a** deceit **which, as** he **observed,** 'he **had not ex-**pected from *him*.'

It *is* hard **to** put it *all* **down in the** schedule, and Jack had hoped to gradually **pay** off his less pressing debts without going through the unpleasant process of 'telling father;' he had in plain English been **guilty of** absolute falsehood, **for,** trusting **to the** forbearance **of** his trades-men, **he had** positively **denied** that he owed a farthing more than the sum he had confessed to. But the **tradesmen were a** faithless and **unconfiding** generation; they **had sent in the bills to his college** tutor, and that gentleman had forwarded them to Squire Armer 'without note or comment.' Hence was the squire very wroth indeed, and still more *grieved* to find in his son a deceit which he despised, and a lie which he hated.

It is very bad for gentlemen of a plethoric habit to give the reins to their tempers, and, as Mr. Armer journeyed swiftly to London, he felt the effects of the stormy scene with his son, in a certain dizziness and singing in the ears, which signs were not without their warnings, insomuch that the squire then and there made up his mind to control himself more strictly for the future. It is, however, one thing to make up one's mind, and quite another thing to abide by such 'makings-up,' and many trials of mind and temper were in store for our poor squire.

To withdraw a large amount of capital from a 'concern' is not, as the showman observed of his show, 'one of those per-

formances at which you go in at one end,
and out at the other, it is a long and
tedious performance;' and so, indeed, did
Mr. Armer find it, for though his soul
loathed the baking and dusty streets of
London, and wended its way in spirit to the
breezy, tree-shaded lawns of his high-placed
Devonshire home, yet here was he compelled to endure daily swelterings over hot
pavements and in pent-up offices with the
thermometer 'anywhere,' to be followed
by sleepless nights in the stuffy chamber
of his hotel. Moreover, this process of
eliminating his capital resulted in an unpleasant kind of ' sweating,' and it began
to dawn upon him that the large income
he had been in the habit of receiving from
the partnership, without too much enquiry
as to the 'how' or the 'whence,' did not
after all represent so very bulky a sum
of money, the astute Gidley having net-
ted and handed over a rate of interest
which in less cunning and careful hands

would have seemed risky in the extreme.

Admiration at his partner's talent for money-spending mingled with his regret at this sudden severance of their relations, a severance, too, for which he felt he only had his own obstinate folly to blame. It was not unnatural, truly, that he should kick against the 'sleeping' character which *his* share of the partnership had been gradually assuming ; but as the truth was now very plainly put before him, and he saw how careful, and, at the same time, how bold when occasion warranted, Gidley had been, he could not but own to himself that it had been better for him had he been a little more patient and more submissive under the irksome control. Gidley, he had to confess to himself, had borne a great deal from *him*, and he now wished with all his heart he had let matters alone, and that the well-known firm of Armer and Gidley were still to the fore on the Stock Exchange.

Nevertherless, when all the partitions and rendings were at an end, there was a goodly sum at Mr. Armer's disposal, and he buckled to his work once more, not without a certain satisfaction, after all, as he felt the old fire of speculation burning up again, and a new life rising in him at the old war-cries of 'rise' and 'fall,' and all the other mysterious rousing-calls of the grand game of finance.

The name of Armer was one tolerably well-known, and where a man has the wherewithal, and the will, and, moreover, a certain amount of skill and experience, there will not want opportunities for the turning-over of his capital, nor folks extremely willing to assist in the operation, with a view to catching such coins as they may the while the money is a-turning; so found the squire, and a very short time after he was rid of Gidley, or rather Gidley was rid of him, Mr. Armer was up to his neck in various enterprises, and the old life at Coombridge was rapidly becoming a pleasant dream of the past.

After the balmy air of Devon, the smoke-laden atmosphere of London was abominable to the quondam country gentleman. Some relief from the stifling streets Mr. Armer felt he *must* have, and hence it came to pass that he cast about to find what he wanted, and eventually found it in a comfortable house in the breezy suburb of Hampstead; and hither did his daughter Nellie hasten very shortly, to go through the unpleasant process of 'settling-in,' leaving the doleful Jack to his own sweet devices at Coombridge.

An empty house, and a long purse from which to draw the supplies to furnish it withal, are, however, tempting baits to a young and energetic woman, and the busy occupation, the running to and fro, the interviews with servants, and with upholsterers, iron-mongers, and the whole tribe of the furnishers was a welcome relief from the anxious thought her concealed engagement brought upon Nellie Armer. Brother Jack was away, and in too dismal a frame of mind to indulge in joking, and she was spared his customary gibes and flouts, which would have been unendurable under the circumstances; but it was pain and grief to her to be so much with her unsuspecting parent, and to feel this embarrassment of concealment between them. All things come to an end, however; even the dilatoriness of the British tradesman has its limits, and it was, at length, with a sigh of relief that Nellie saw the last van pass out of sight down the leafy lane leading from the heath, in which Heathfield, as the Armers' house was called, was placed.

'Well, Nellie,' said Mr. Armer, as they moved into the drawing-room together after the first dinner at Heathfield with any elements of comfort about it, 'who would have believed three months ago that we should be back again in smoky London?'

' Of course it is not Coombridge, father,' said Nellie, ' but it is quiet, and even pretty, and not so smoky after all, though the flowers *are* a little grimy, and the grass not calculated to improve a white gown if one reclines upon it unsuspicious of evil : I found that out this morning under our tree—imagine having only one tree to boast of !'

' Never mind, Nellie, I don't intend to live here for ever, and when I have made a little more for you and Jack (though *he* doesn't deserve it, the young rascal !) we will go back to Coombridge and " live happily ever after." '

' Why should you ever have left Coombridge, father ?' asked Nellie ; ' it will be a frightful expense the keeping up both places.'

' Because, my dear, your father is not so rich as he was ; in fact, I fear I shall have to let Coombridge ; but, any rate, I shall keep it on till the summer is over.

There is plenty of hunting of a sort
there, the shooting is good, and the Teign
is close by, so I shall easily let the place,
I hope.' But the sigh, with which the
squire's sentence ended, gave a portentous
denial to his 'hope,' and Nellie knew that
her father was even now turning a fond
and longing backward glance to his old
haunts and occupations.

A long pause in the conversation en-
sued, during which both Nellie and her
father were busily employed with the
thoughts of their old home: he, with the
coverts, and the ' birds ' that dwell therein,
with side thoughts as to the wily coney,
and much exercisings as to what Master
Bailey, the keeper, was after, and as to
when he could snatch a few days to run
down and 'have a slap at 'em;' and she,
with a certain nobleman residing at a
'reasonable distance' from her home, and
of whose approaching advent in London—
and at Heathfield also, rest well assured—

she was advised during their last meeting
just before she left for London.

Twice had they met since the fateful
day at Coombridge : once under the Argus
eyes of Lady Limborne, who was making
one of her rare calls upon 'those roturiers'
at Coombridge, and once again when Lord
Limborne rode over to dine with Jack, and
condole with that erring person upon what
he was pleased to call his 'cussed luck.'
In a party of three (for the squire was in
London) it is difficult sometimes to get
rid of the one who is 'not company,' but a
few minutes the lovers managed to snatch
whilst Master Jack was superintending
the lighting up of the billiard-table, and in
that brief space Lord Limborne hurriedly
informed Nellie that he had had, as yet, no
favourable opportunity to broach *the* subject—of their engagement, to wit—with his
mother, while Nellie informed him of her
whereabouts in Hampstead, whereupon he
remarked that business of a most urgent

nature, namely, the desire to see his beloved, would call him up to the great metropolis at no distant date . . . here Jack's voice was heard calling to them, and the meeting was reluctantly dissolved.

'Nellie,' said Mr. Armer, waking up at last from the reverie which has given us the opportunity of this unpardonably long digression, and showing by his first remark that his thoughts, towards the end of the aforesaid reverie, had taken a less pleasant turn—'Nellie, I have been thinking about your brother Jack; his deceit has been a very painful blow to me.'

'Oh, father,' cried Nellie, standing up for her dearly-loved brother, 'don't call it by such a hard name as that! Lord Limborne says that almost all young men run into debt at college, and are afraid to tell, or perhaps don't even know, all the truth about it.'

'I don't know,' said the squire, 'what Lord Limborne has to do with it, and I

am sorry the nasty business has gone out
of the family.   I suppose the young idiot
was confiding his troubles and whining
about them to his friend ?'

Nellie did not inform her parent that she
also was a delinquent, and had discussed
the 'nasty business' in solemn conference
with the two friends.

'One thing,' Mr. Armer went on, 'I am
resolved upon, and that is he shall not go
to the Bar as I intended : I should only
have the same disgraceful worries over
again. No, I shall keep him under my own
eye, and he shall come into my office.   I
don't suppose Jack will ever be a business
man, but this will keep him occupied and
out of mischief, at any rate.   I wish now I
had never sent him to that abominable
"Varsity," as he calls it; he is just the last
person to be trusted to the tender mercies
of confiding tradesmen. What do *you*
think about it, Nellie ?'

Now Nellie knew that the very thought

of offices, high stools, musty ledgers, and the rest of it was abhorrent to her brother, who had always looked forward to spending his days as a country squire, and who, next to his sister and his father, loved his horse, his dogs, and guns more than all other things upon this earth; and, knowing this, her father's question put her into a quandary from which she escaped by mildly remarking that 'she did not think Jack would like London; she thought he was more suited to a country life.'

'Perhaps,' said Mr. Armer, 'some day he may come to that; for, of course, he will have the place when I am gone; but, in the meantime, he *must* do something, for I don't intend him to idle away his time, and get into debt again.' Here Mr. Armer rose, and kissing his daughter bade her good-night, and wended his way to his own den to smoke the pipe of peace and look over the evening papers before retiring to rest.

CHAPTER X.

IN SOLEMN CONCLAVE.

IT is a great mistake to suppose that the 'putting on of side' (to use a somewhat slangy expression) is confined to the higher walks of society. To the student of human nature, it quickly becomes revealed that while *all* ranks of life delight in this vulgar exercise, while Her Grace the Duchess bestows two fingers in greeting her humble parasite and admirer, and while at the other end of the rope the costermonger's lady whose husband is the proud possessor of his own 'moke' looks down with something like contempt upon the lady whose lord and master is forced by unkind Fortune to trundle his barrow himself—

while these two extremes meet upon this
common platform of Pride, it is to the
middle classes of our community that we
must look to find this evil weed flourishing
in its proudest luxuriance. Here the very
remotest 'connection with the aristocracy'
becomes a valuable and marketable social commodity, and the he or she who
can claim cousinship with a dilapidated
baronet, or still better with an out-at-
elbows or even disreputable peer, is not
slow in proclaiming this important fact,
and in exacting the full social value therefor : while, if a cruel Fate should attach
even the faintest aroma of 'trade' to the
social aspirant, heavens! with what pains
is the shocking taint concealed; not even
the 'touch of the tar-brush' is more carefully painted over and hidden out of sight
in democratic America. Absolute truthfulness is not very possible in the ·face of
hints, and more or less delicate enquiries
on this subject, and denials must be given,

even where such denials are, in plain English, lies; for a man may keep a store in Australia, or New Zealand, or Timbuctoo; he may sell (strictly at the other end of the world) even disgusting articles of commerce; he may positively *revel* in trade, and purvey all manner of things from the mild and useful pill of Cockle to an up-and-down suit of go-to-meeting clothes; he may keep a butcher's shop; he may deal in raw skins —and return to his native Britain refulgent with the golden profits, and be 'received' into society with open arms, particularly if he be of a sociable disposition, and show a desire to disburse his gains in laudable efforts to amuse and entertain his fellow-creatures. But let a butcher of even gigantic wealth—as butchers there be in these halcyon (strictly for butchers) days of unheard-of, not to say painful, prices— let a purveyor of meat, as he loved to be called, whose name was proudly displayed in letters of gold over his emporium (how

vulgar is the word 'shop!') in say the
Buckingham Palace Road—let such an one
retire with his 'plum,' his hundred thousand
pounds, and take a 'place in the country,'
and not a soul (of the 'quality') will enter
his gates, be they opened never so widely;
and not till two or three generations have
sufficed to wash out the smell of the shop
will his descendants be admitted to the
second-rate society of the 'county,' and
that not without flouts and secret gibings.
Is the beef of Brisbane, or is the mutton of
Manitoba, less vulgarising than the flesh of
the beeves and sheep of Old England?
These things are a mystery!

Problems of society hingeing upon such
matters as 'Who to know?' and 'Who to
drop?' were mightily exercising the mind
of that determined stormer of social heights,
Mrs. Denton. It was getting on towards
the period in summer when that sluggish
stream, society in Devon, is wont to be
quickened by certain freshets and flushes

in the shape of balls, dinner-parties, and melancholy entertainments yclept ' at homes,' and Mrs. Denton was alive to the opportunities this festive time might afford her.

Now, the results of that bold free-lance, Miss Charlotte Ingle's, determined attacks at Teignbridge were pleasantly evident at Wreford in a quite respectable array of trophies in the shape of visiting cards ; cards inscribed, too, with the names of persons of some distinction in the county, and these were the *avant-couriers* of invitations to sundry social gatherings, of which the Dentons were not slow to avail themselves.

Verily the blissful visions of the wife, son, and daughters of the homely master of Wreford seemed in a fair way to become realities ; the outworks were already taken, and, although the sacred precincts of *the* set had not as yet been invaded, crafty approaches thereto were being constructed, and diplomatic relations were being opened.

It was in the mind of the bold Mrs. Denton to give a ball, a grand and sumptuous entertainment, the like whereof had never yet been seen in the county of Devon, and at which should be assembled all (as the county papers called them) the élite of the county; and to procure the presence and countenance of those who still held aloof from Wreford and the inhabitants thereof, and at the same time to weed out the now useless friends (?) from an already too large visiting-list—these were tasks which called for larger powers than Mrs. Denton or her children possessed.

Gratitude for past favours, and a lively sense of favours to come, coupled with a knowledge, from experience, of her boldness in attack, and her high intelligence in the science of 'Who is who?' pointed at once to the energetic Miss Ingle as the *confidante* and agent; and it was for these so high and lofty purposes that a solemn conclave was being held in Mrs. Denton's boudoir one morning late in July, at which the whole family 'assisted,' with the fair Charlotte as 'guide, philosopher, and friend.'

'Seems like a court of law, with Tresa there with her paper and pens, and mother with her visiting-book, and us all sitting round so solemn-like,' said Mr. Denton, who had refused to be shut out, though told 'he need not trouble,' and was much impressed with the occasion. 'Anyone 'd think it was a trial for murder, instead of a ball.'

'I wish you would not say such dreadful things, father; you quite shock Miss Ingle,' said Theresa, who, as her father remarked, 'was always a-badgering and a-bullying him.'

'It would take a great deal more than that to shock *me*,' said Miss Ingle, with perfect truthfulness, 'and we certainly do look like a solemn assembly.'

'Oh! it is quite too exciting! only to

think of the *piles* of people we know; and
what *fun* to leave out all the **odious ones.**
Let us begin at once. **Now** then, Henry,
for heaven's sake look a little more lively.'
Thus the beautiful Theresa roused to en-
thusiasm, and exasperated at her brother,
who **was** reclining in an elegant attitude
in **a** cushioned embrasure of a window,
and sniffing in **a most** aggravatingly nonchalant **air at a** pale-yellow rose.

'It is a matter of but small moment **to**
me,' replied the flaccid Henry. '**I care**
but little for these **trivialities—nay, I dis-**
like them; they disturb the **even flow of**
thought, so necessary **for the** creation of
poesy.'

'For goodness **sake, then, go back to**
that æsthetic den of yours, **and "live up"**
to something, or do another verse or two
of those wonderful **poems of** yours **of**
which **we** hear so much, and **see so** little;
this kind of thing, as **you say, is** quite too
gross **for poets and** blighted ones,' retorted

Theresa, who had but scant sympathy with her brother's 'fiddle-faddles,' as she elegantly called his æsthetic pursuits, and the adjuncts thereto.

Now was wrath seen upon the usually impassive face of the heir of Wreford, and one of the not infrequent wrangles between brother and sister would certainly have raged had not Mrs. Denton called her quarrelsome offspring to order.

'I do think, Theresa,' she said, 'you might cease teasing Henry, and interrupting everything in this way; you ought really to control yourself, and be less temperish.'

'Temperish!' exclaimed Theresa, not to be put down. 'Henry is enough to provoke a saint, with his airs, and graces, and pack of rubbish; I've no patience with him!'

'It is my fate to be misunderstood, dear mother,' said Henry, with a faint sigh. 'I will not wrangle; it is exhausting and vulgar;' and, with this passing shot at his

sister, he sank into the comfortable em-
brace of a well-cushioned settee, unheeding
the snort of contempt with which his sister
greeted his remark as she tossed her head
and glared at her submissive adversary.

"'Oighty-toighty! 'ere's a fine way of
setting about the ball,' cried Mr. Denton;
'whatever are you two always fighting
and snarling about? Haven't you got
everything to make you 'appy? Tresa
with her dresses and a fine maid to wait
upon her, and me a-giving of her any
mortial thing as she likes to arsk for, and
'Enery with his chaney, and his books,
and all them expensive things as he's
always buying? You ought to be
ashamed of yourselves, I tell you. All
right, mother! I'm done; but I must
say, all the same, it's disgustin', ain't it,
now, Miss Ingle?'

'You certainly are a most indulgent
father to your children, Mr. Denton,' said
Miss Ingle, 'and I am sure they are grate-

ful; but we really must begin, if we are to
do anything, or we never shall get through
this affair. Do you know, Mrs. Denton,'
turning to her hostess, 'I have been thinking it would be a great thing for you in the
county if you could get Lady Limborne to
come on the 27th. So many of the best
people think so much of her, don't you
know, and some of those we are not quite
sure of would be certain to come if it were
given out that she is to be here.'

'I am sure I wish we *could* get her,'
said Mrs. Denton, 'but she is so stand-
offish; we have met her once or twice since
you introduced us at Teignbridge, and she
will hardly take any notice of us at all. I
don't see what we can do; perhaps you can
think of something?'

'Stand-offish!' exclaimed Mr. Denton,
'1 should think so; why, she reg'lar turned her back on us at that tennis turna-
mong, as you call it, at Burford. I was
just saying, " How d'ye do, my lady?" when

she turned right round, and began to talk
to some party or other, as if she never
saw me ; *course* she saw me,—a dead cut,
that's what it was. If you ask me, I say,
leave the proud old cat alone ; I 'ate such
airs.'

'Mr. Denton,' said his wife, solemnly,
'it is dreadful to hear you talk in such a
way of a lady of title. I am astonished
at you.'

'Well, well! do as you like, my dear,
do as you like ; if you *prefer* to be snubbed
and trodden on, *I* shan't interfere : anyway,
you can't *make* her civil, which civil she
certainly ain't.'

'I think,' said Miss Ingle, who had been
impatiently drumming on the table with
her pencil, whilst this little interlude went
on, 'I think that something might be
done, only it's a little delicate, and would
require careful handling.'

'If anyone can do it, it is you, Charlotte,' said her admirer Theresa ; and Mr.

Denton, his spouse, and Emily leant forward to listen, while even the abstracted Henry looked up from the book he was pretending to read, to hear the plan by which the haughty Lady Limborne was to be subdued, and brought a captive to the Wreford ball.

'Well, I will tell you my plan,' said Miss Ingle, 'I have been thinking a great deal about it, for it is very important for you to get Lady Limborne here on the 27th, and this is the plan I have hit upon. Have you ever seen Limborne Church?'

'Limborne Church?' cried Emily, and all the rest of the audience looked astonished; 'why, whatever can that have to do with us and Lady Limborne?'

'Listen,' said the oracle, quite in her element, 'and you shall soon hear. Limborne Church is one of the most ancient churches in the diocese, and has quite the most lovely carved screen in the county. The living belongs to the Limborne family, and the chancel is quite full of their monuments and things; but the church is in a most dreadful state of dilapidation—it looks as if it were tumbling to pieces, and is quite a disgrace. Of course Lord Limborne and Lady Limborne are most anxious to have the church put in order, and Lord Limborne has stirred up the old rector to set a subscription-list going; well! they have got the money all but about two hundred and fifty pounds, and only the other day Lady Limborne was speaking to me about it, and I thought of you at once. She asked me however people got so many churches restored, and said how much she wished to see Limborne Church in decent order.'

'Oh! I think I could tell her ladyship something about *that*,' interpolated Mr. Denton, 'talk about beggars! I never saw anything like these parsons; why, there's 'ardly a day passes but one or other of 'em writes to me, a-buttering me up first, and

begging after. Whenever I see something
or other rectory or vicarage a-top of a
letter, *I* know what's coming—"well-known
benevolence," "justly earned title for
generosity," "duties of wealth," and "kindly assist with a cheque." Lor' anyone 'd
think I was *made* of money, like that
Crœsis, or whatever you call it.'

'I am sure, Mr. Denton,' said Miss Ingle,
'it is because everybody knows how
generous you are.'

'Well, I'm blest if you ain't going on
the same way, Miss Ingle. I didn't think it
of *you*. Let 'em restore their church themselves, and not go bothering other folks. I
suppose her ladyship has put you up to get
some money out of me; a likely story, after
the way she's treated us;' and Mr. Denton
shook his head in a most determined manner.

'Hush!' said his more astute spouse,
'you need not speak so fiercely to Miss
Ingle. I think I begin to see something of
what she means.'

'Well, I can't say I do,' said Mr. Denton, 'unless those Limbornes want me to do their restoring-job for them; and whatever that's got to do with getting the old lady here is more than I can tell. I'm sure *I* don't want her, anyhow.'

'It has *all* to do with it,' said Charlotte Ingle; 'and, if you are willing to give them a handsome cheque towards this work, I think I can promise that Lady Limborne shall be here on the 27th.'

'Well! of all the cool . . . . you don't mean to tell me, Miss Ingle, that I am to *pay* my lady for coming here? I tell you I don't want her, I'll see her . . . .'

'Wait a minute, father,' hastily interrupted Theresa, who knew that her mother had other views, besides the social weight Lady Limborne's presence carried with it, in wishing to get upon terms with that lady, and who was not unmindful of the importance to her own ambitious schemes that this plan of Miss Ingle's might betoken.

'Do wait a minute like a dear, good, old father.'

'Ah! Miss, you're after something or other, or you wouldn't be so softy. I ain't a-going to be caught with chaff like that, don't you fear,' rejoined Theresa's parent.

'Now, Henry, how *can* you talk like that, my dear?' said Mrs. Denton, in quite dulcet tones. 'I am sure Theresa is quite right if she *does* want you to help Lady Limborne: it *is* very important to us to be friendly with her, and whatever does a cheque matter to *you*. You put matters so . . . . so . . . . plainly, my dear; what can be the *harm* of helping Lady Limborne to restore her church? You are always giving away money when it isn't the least use to us. I don't often ask you to do anything of the sort, and I think you *might* give way this once; after all, it is for a good object.'

'Good object! yes, they're *all* "good objects,"' growled Mr. Denton, with a

sardonic grin; 'but I don't want to be
nasty about it, and, if you're all so particular about it, I won't stand at a hunderd or
two, so there! I'll just write a cheque
to-day, and send it with my compliments.'

'If you *do*,' said Charlotte Ingle, 'you
will spoil everything, and the cheque will
probably be sent back by return of post.'

'Whatever *do* you want me to do, then?'
was Mr. Denton's question. '*I* can't make
you out, all of you; first, you say my lady
wants a cheque for two hundred and fifty
pounds, and then you say she'll send it
back if I send one, it's ridicklus!'

'Allow me, Mr. Denton, to explain,'
said Miss Ingle. 'I am sorry I did not
make myself clear; of course the cheque,
if you are good enough to give one, must
be sent to the Rector of Limborne for the
Restoration Fund; of course, too, he will
at once run up to the Castle with the news,
for he knows how anxious Lady Limborne
is on the subject, and she, I am sure, can-

not feel anything but grateful to you for your generosity.'

'Very well, then, settle it your own way, though I think it is one of the most bare-faced . . . . well, I don't know what to call it, and that's a fact! Live and learn! Live and learn! that's my motter since I came into brother Ben's money; go on, go on, what's the next article?' said Mr. Denton, who was to have other lessons as to the market value of social prestige.

'My *dear* Henry, what a way you have of speaking,' exclaimed Mrs. Denton, with a shuddering remembrance of the 'shop' which her husband's last words called up. 'And now, girls,' she went on, addressing her daughters, who had been silent but attentive assistants at the 'pumping' of their father, 'the next matter for us to arrange is—who are we to ask? and—who are we to leave out? I have a list here; Theresa, my dear, just hand me that list. You see, Charlotte, when we first came here we did

not know anything about the people, and
of course we have made some rather
unfortunate acquaintances.'

'We was glad enough to know anyone,
and that's the truth, as you know, my
dear; and there *were* some rum 'uns at our
first Al Fresky. I never shall forget how
some of those Bardon folks did walk into
the victuals, and drink; anyone'd a-thought
they'd been starving theirselves a purpose;'
and Mr. Denton laughed loudly at the
remembrance.

'Oh! of course you cannot know the
Bardon people, it is a dreadful place,' said
Miss Ingle, 'there is not a single person
there that anyone knows; it is a kind of
city of refuge for all sorts of queer
people—people who have been in Queer
Street, don't you know, and that kind of
thing. I am told the drinking that goes
on there is quite too dreadful, and I can
easily believe what Mr. Denton says about
them.'

'I am *so* glad you told us,' said Mrs. Denton, ' we will strike them all out ;' and struck out they were.

Here Mr. Denton, junior, who was tired of the conversation, rose, and sauntered out of the room, quickly followed by his father, and the ladies were left to the congenial occupation of sifting the visiting-list, and discussing the social positions and the shortcomings of their friends.

CHAPTER XI.

NEWS FOR LADY LIMBORNE.

LORD LIMBORNE was finding out the truth of the ancient proverb that tells us 'Honesty is the best policy.' Limborne Castle was in a most unwonted state of turmoil. The old butler confided to the venerable abigail who was at the head of the feminine departments the fact that 'he was most worritted to death; he never minded sich goings-on since the time when he was footboy, and the old lord brought home her ladyship, and a fine figure of a woman she were.'

Truly the long sleep of many years was broken at last; such furbishings-up of time-worn furniture, such scrubbing, airing, and setting in order of long unoccupied rooms—the whole place seemed alive once more, and the noise and bustling were all the more strange from the quiet that had reigned there so long. ' Such goings-on,' indeed ! A cook from London, ' on the job,' caused a perfect revolution in the kitchen, and reduced the old Devonshire crone who usually presided there to a state of semi-idiotcy ; ' her ladyship was witched, sure enough,' she said, ' a-puttin' out her money in such ways ; well, it wasn't for the likes of *her* to spake ill of her betters, but she know'd her was mazed, for certain.' Her ladyship was anything but ' mazed,' however ; she was in very complete possession of her noble wits, and was only acting upon the homely proverb which speaks of the wisdom of ' risking a sprat to catch a whale.'

All this unwonted disbursing of exceedingly scanty cash was, it may well be imagined, not without some object, and that object was only too well revealed to her son. The Beldons were expected for a short stay at the Castle. In vain had Lord Limborne exhausted himself in arguments, trying to show to his mother the absurdity of asking people to stay at Limborne Castle whose ordinary life was so very differently mounted from the quiet and even tenor of the Limborne way; in vain did he descant upon the folly of spending money, so much wanted in so many ways, in the useless display involved in this attempt to entertain such very exalted personages. Lady Limborne was determined, and there was an end of the matter.

Now Lord Limborne had had neither the time, inclination, nor money to mingle much in the society to which his rank would have given him the easy *entrée*, and he had therefore scarcely seen Emily Beldon since the time when, as a gawky maiden of sixteen, she had paid his mother a visit at the Castle. During the interval she had developed into a very fine young lady indeed: tall and shapely, stately in her carriage, with a beautiful face, somewhat marred by its expression of extreme haughtiness, the proud Lady Emily was not unlike Lord Limborne's mother in person, while in character, aims, and views the two aristocratic dames were completely at one. It was not strange, therefore, that Lady Limborne should see in such a congenial character the person best fitted to mate with her son; and when the high political influence of the lady's father, and the great wealth that must accrue to his only child were taken into consideration, the proposed alliance seemed in every way so desirable that it is no wonder the prospect dazzled Lady Limborne, and the furtherance of the arrangement became a sort of monomania with her.

Although no direct intimation of the true object of this visit to Devonshire had been

given to the person most concerned, yet
certain hints had fallen from her mother.
Lord Limborne's praise had been judicious-
ly sounded, and the brilliant future to
which his undoubted talents, and his
powerful connections clearly pointed, had
not failed of due discussion ; while, on *her*
part, the mother of the supposed *prétend-
ant* had paid the daughter-in-law of her
choice little attentions and courtesies
which, together with much talk about the
many excellencies of her own son, served
plainly enough to point out her wishes in
the matter.

Various causes conspired to incline the
high and mighty damsel to listen to the
voice of the charmer: her people seemed
disposed towards the alliance; she ad-
mired Lord Limborne's reputation, she
liked him also personally, she could 'get
on' excellently with his mother, and she
felt that her position as the daughter of a
powerful and very rich nobleman could not

be better used than in furthering the ambitions of a clever and talented man, and
in bringing new life into an ancient and
impoverished line.

Besides these weighty reasons, there
was another spur, if one were wanted, to
urge her to a favourable entertaining of
Lord Limborne's pretensions. An uneasy
sense of failure would sometimes make
itself to be felt in her 'inner conscious-
ness.' Already two seasons had she been
'out,' and she had not received that attention to which, as she very strongly felt,
her person and position entitled her; in
truth, there was something repellent in
her proud manners, something hard, too,
in her cold, haughty face, beautiful as it
undoubtedly was, and one would almost
as soon have thought of making love to a
magnificent example of the sculptor's art
as to the proud daughter of the Earl of
Beldon.

These extremely proud folk are human

enough, **after all, and it was** sufficiently
mortifying to the Lady Emily **to see** maidens fair of very much less degree, beauty,
and riches the centres of attraction, **while**
the possessor of so many and evident advantages was left, comparatively speaking,
out in the cold. Neither did Lady Emily
care for '**the** modern young **man ;**' she
despised the ' chic,' **the slangy tone, and**
general fastness of tone and manner which
alone seemed able to please **the** ' Johnnies
and Chappies,' and **she was ready to find
in** the somewhat grave demeanour **of Lord**
Limborne a relief from the frivolous chat-
ter of the society young man ; and, after a
proper interval, she felt not indisposed **to**
accept **him** as a companion in those cold
and lofty regions of life in which she intended to dwell.

It **is,** however, a question whether—our
little heroine, Nellie, to the contrary, notwithstanding—Lord Limborne would ever
have brought himself to this arrangement

with all its manifold advantages. There
are many exceptions to that venerable rule
that 'Like mates most easily with like,'
so many, in fact, that these exceptions
may almost be said to have become the
rule. While the man small of stature
seeks the tall and stately damsel as his
mate, and walks contentedly beside her
with the crown of his abnormally tall hat
on a level with the strings of her bonnet,
and while, on the other hand, the giant
among men proceeds upon *his* way with a
little elf of a woman just tall enough to
be able to hook her tiny hand into his
elbow-joint; while dark mates with light,
the blonde seeking the brunette, and
brown eyes looking for love into blue
eyes,—so it falls out also with character
and disposition; the irritable genius seeks,
naturally enough, for repose and rest of
mind in the comely house-wife, proud of
her husband, but not in the least under-
standing his flights of fancy, or, more

melancholy still, his brilliant wit and
humour.   The lymphatic disposition seeks
what is wanting in his or her character in
the nervous.   And so it comes to pass that
we see so many strangely-assorted couples,
and are so constantly asking one another,
'What on earth So-and-so could see to like
in Mrs. So-and-so?' and 'However that
clever fellow What's-his-name could have
thrown himself away upon that most unin-
tersting of women Mrs. What-her-name?'

Whatever may be the rights of these
rules and exceptions above descanted upon,
certain it is that Lord Limborne found
himself involved in a very painful predicament indeed, and regretted very earnestly his folly in not insisting more strongly against his mother's matrimonial designs
for him at the first hints of those designs.
He had not come under the glamour of the
fair Helen Armer then, and had treated
Lady Limborne's plans in anything but a
serious humour.   However, the tables were

turned upon him now with a vengeance,
and the joke was becoming very unpleas-
antly in earnest.

This 'forced march' of Lady Limborne's,
this bringing down the noble army of
Beldon to the attack, compelled him to
make suddenly an announcement he had
hoped to soften by a gradual disclosure.
If he could have persuaded his mother
of the hopelessness of any attempt thus
arbitrarily to arrange his future for him;
if, when she had well digested this impossibility, he could make her understand
that, in the matter of Nellie, his happiness
was really at stake; he had felt it would
have been possible for him to overcome
Lady Limborne's opposition to such a
match—at any rate, in such a way as to
gain for his *inamorita* if not an effusive,
yet a sufficiently graceful, reception. Now,
however, with the unpleasantness of the
last few weeks between them, with the
Beldon element thus plainly displayed, the

awkwardness of the affair accentuated by
the presence of the 'parties affected,' he
felt dismally *certain* that Lady Limborne
would flatly refuse to receive his Nellie as
a prospective daughter-in-law ; that, even
if he could prevail over Nellie, her father
would most assuredly resent any slight to
his dearly-loved daughter—and, in short,
the whole business was a painful and intricate one; and he wished with all his
heart he had 'bided a wee,' and not 'disclosed his pains' until these Beldon com-
plications should be cleared away, and his
mother more ready to resign herself to the
inevitable. Still he could not let the Beldons come to the Castle without letting
Lady Limborne know that his affections
were otherwise engaged; and not until the
evening before the arrival of these important persons did he screw up his courage
for what he knew must be a painful interview with his mother.

After a *tête-à-tête* dinner, accompanied

with conversation of a spasmodic and con-
strained sort, instead of going off to his
den to smoke the post-prandial cigarette,
according to his wont, he followed his
mother into her drawing-room.

Lady Limborne looked up from her work
with a questioning air, slightly astonished
to see her son before the tea was announced
to him in his study.

'I . . . . I wanted to speak to you,
mother,' said he, hesitatingly, and wondering how he could best make the announcement he had to make. 'I want to speak
to you about these Beldons.'

'I do not see what more you can have to
say to me, James, about this most unfortunate affair, unless you are willing to do as
I wish, and as is certainly best for *you*. I
cannot help resenting the predicament I
am placed in,' said Lady Limborne, going
off at full speed into the region of her
grievances; 'it is most awkward. If you
had given me the least hint of your un-

accountable dislike to Emily, you would have spared me much humiliation.'

'I do not in the least dislike Emily Beldon, mother. How should I? Why, I have scarcely seen anything of her since she was little more than a child; I know hardly anything of her.'

'Then why do you so obstinately set yourself against her? Why, when I have taken so much trouble, and when there are so many advantages, do you determine to oppose my strong wishes?'

'But, mother, how can you know what Emily Beldon's feelings—to say nothing of mine for the moment—may be in the matter? Why should you suppose that she is ready to rush into my arms in this impetuous manner? I feel sure you are mistaken altogether. Why on earth should she want to marry *me*, of all people in the world, who never yet paid her the slightest attention? The very idea is ridiculous.'

'It is not at all ridiculous, James; I

have told you before, and I tell you again, that I do not believe you would have any difficulty in the matter; she has no other entanglement—I took care to ascertain this; she is quite aware that her people and that I would be pleased with such an arrangement; she has spoken of you in such a way that I am sure she admires your reputation, and so forth; and where *can* you find a wife more suited to you in *every way?* Unless you have some other attachment,—which I cannot believe, for you would surely have spoken to me about it,—unless there is some one else, I cannot conceive why you hesitate. You allowed me to take some steps in the matter, you cannot say I acted without your knowledge, and I must say again I feel acutely the position your unaccountable change has placed me in; it is so unlike you, too, James.'

'But, mother, you must surely acknowledge that a man, even if Lady Emily were ——oh! it is *too* absurd! A man cannot

force his feelings and affections, and com-
pel himself to marry **to order!**'

'That is a very vulgar way of speaking,
James; of course people in our position
cannot marry like shop-people and clerks;
noblesse oblige, and I think **it** is your *duty*
to, at any rate, try to like Emily Beldon. I
do not wish to speak **again** upon the subject, **it is an** extremely distasteful one to
me; you have only yourself to blame; and
when **I** consider the painfulness of the explanation I *must* have with Lady Beldon,
unless you prove **to be the sensible man**
and **the** kind son you have always been
until now; it is more than **I can** bear;
if you are obstinate, and force **me to**
go through this ordeal, I think, at least,
you might spare me your reproaches.'
A truly feminine speech on her ladyship's
part, **for the** much-worried James had
never reproached his mother at all; and it
is a familiar **manœuvre of 'the sex,'** moreover, **this of assuming injuries** never
intended or even dreamed of.

Lord Limborne was leaning against the mantelpiece, looking down upon his mother, nervously gnawing his moustaches the while ; for the time had come, and the fell announcement must be made at once.

'Mother,' he said, after a short pause, in which he was trying to marshal his ideas, and to soften the blow, 'mother, you said just now something about another attachment.'

Lady Limborne looked up at her son with a face of keen inquiry.

'Yes,' she said, 'I did. I cannot believe . . . it cannot be that you . . . .'

' Mother,' he said, going over to her and standing by her chair, uncertain how to act—' mother, I was wrong not to tell you of this before. I thought all this foolishness about the Beldons was anything but the serious affair you have made it, and I did not begin to think so much about Nellie until after you had gone ; I did not mean to *say* anything to her until I had spoken to you——' and he was going on thus, in a confused search after excuses, when Lady Limborne interrupted him.

'Nellie!' she cried—'you cannot mean Helen Armer? It cannot be the daughter of those people at Coombridge?'

'I ought to have told you before,' said her son, quietly and coldly, for he was stung by the accent of contempt with which his mother mentioned 'those people' —'I ought to have told you before that I have asked Nellie Armer to marry me, and that she has accepted me.'

'So I should have imagined,' returned Lady Limborne, with a sneer; 'it was tolerably certain that Mr. Armer's daughter would be persuaded to accept Lord Limborne. I am obliged to my son for the honour he proposes to do me in bringing the Armers into the pedigree of the Hautfords and the Limbornes. And may I ask how long this interesting romance has been going on?'

Intense pride of birth and position has in it something of vulgarity, and we are not unfrequently surprised to discover a vein of the vulgar even in the polished marble of the very loftiest; nay, these lofty personages themselves, far removed, as they are taught to conceive themselves to be, from the faults of that common herd who are 'not in society,' and infinitely above what they regard as 'the lower orders,' or 'the masses,' do occasionally display a power of invective, for instance, which would have done credit to Billingsgate in the very palmiest days of that malodorous market. If not in the *words* of the brawny fish-fags, yet in the same *spirit* does the 'give and take' proceed; the weapons are polished to quite a dazzling brightness, and the manœuvrings of the combat are conducted with more of finesse, but the weapons, rusty or bright, are the same old weapons, and the battle, whether it be fought in my lady's drawing-room or in my lady's kitchen, is very much the same sort of battle too. This is again one of those touches of nature which make the whole world kin, and show us how very much alike we all are when once the trappings are taken off.

Now Lady Limborne could see nothing vulgar in her attempts to get some grip upon the Beldon money and influence, but she was extremely well alive to the vulgarity of a common quarrel; the raised tone of voice, the coarse sneer, the retort uncourteous—all these things were foreign and offensive to her; but this downfall of her most cherished hopes, this sudden end to all her ambitions, was too much for her haughtiness; her cold reserve was a shield not solid enough to keep off such hurtling darts as these, and even in the heat of her disappointment and consequent anger, she was astonished at the odd sound of her own voice raised above its natural pitch, and employed in harsh and unaccustomed sneering.

Lord Limborne was, on his part, so startled at the change in his cold, proud mother, such a shock did her unwontedly loud tones give him, that he failed to answer her, and it was not until her question was repeated that he replied :

'I spoke to Miss Armer at the last Teignbridge,' he said, 'but I have thought of Nellie for some time . . .'

Something in the tone with which he said 'Nellie,' some slight, unconscious lingering over the syllables as if he liked to form them, stung Lady Limborne beyond endurance.

'It is more than I can bear,' she cried, passionately, rising hastily and interrupting him. 'I will *not* bear it !' and her ladyship positively stamped with her foot. 'I refuse absolutely to acknowledge this— this person as my daughter ! I will never receive her ! It is monstrous ! The very idea is repulsive to me !'

'Stop, mother!' exclaimed Lord Limborne. 'Do not say in this heat things that neither of us can forget; you must remember that I love her, and that one day she will be my wife.'

'Never my daughter! Never my daughter!' cried his mother. 'It is the most palpable vulgar scheme, a plot to get your title, James; how *can* you be so blind? All these visits to that detestable place, all the friendship of the odious father and brother, all parts of one wretched plot against you, my poor boy; can you not see it?'

'Mother,' cried Lord Limborne, losing all control over himself at these open charges of scheming against Nellie and her people, 'mother, you dared not to say such things if you knew the Armers as I know them; they are utterly incapable of such vulgar schemes;' and, as his mother smiled as if in pity for his blind folly, he went on, 'and I must say that you are the last person to speak of scheming;

have I not suffered enough already from *your* scheming; yes! I *will* say it, the Armers are incapable of such schemes as we have had here. Is it not scheming this persuading the Beldons into the match you so kindly propose for me? Even if the Armers *had* planned; and manœuvred to secure me for their daughter and sister, it could not have been worse than . . . but I will spare you. I tell you Mr. Armer is so proud that if he had the least hint of this absurd suspicion of yours, if he knew you looked down upon his daughter in this way, he would rather see her in her grave than married to me. But I am wrong to speak to you in this way, mother; forgive me, I lost command over myself, and you are angry and disappointed at first. I feared it would be so; but as time goes on and you see how much in earnest I am, you will be kind to Nellie, for my sake ?' and he went over and tried to take his mother's hand.

'I am indeed shocked and grieved at the way in which you have permitted yourself to speak to me,' said Lady Limborne, availing herself of that common stratagem in feminine warfare, which consists in provoking a man beyond endurance, and then coming down heavily upon him for the unguarded words he utters in his wrath. 'I tell you frankly,' she went on, 'I shall oppose this most unfortunate infatuation of yours with all my power, for I regard such an alliance as meaning little less than social ruin for you. I should consider it an unpardonable fault in myself were I to do otherwise than oppose you.' And with these words Lady Limborne retired from the field of battle with all the honours of war, and before her son had time to reply, leaving that son in no enviable frame of mind.

When Lady Limborne found herself in her own room, she quickly dismissed the aged abigail who waited upon her, and,

too much moved to sit still, she paced up
and down the room, trying to calm herself
and to face this new turn in her affairs
quietly. A strong feeling of disappointment embittered her against the unfortunate Nellie, more sorely than the wounds
to her pride and affection of which the said
Nellie was the innocent cause; for Lady
Limborne had had, in spite of all her son
could say, a feeling of certainty that he
would give way at last; that at last, too,
he would not fail to see Emily Beldon as *she*
saw her, that the manifest advantages of
such an alliance would prevail with him in
the end, and that the marriage would be
arranged if not at this imminent visit, yet
at no very distant period. Even now she
would not despair.

'Surely James,' she thought, 'would not
give out this entanglement of his at once?
if she could only gain time!' And as she
went on thinking deeply over this knotty
point, her son's angry words about the

pride of Mr. Armer came into her mind
with a sudden illumination. 'Certainly
she would *not* receive the daughter ;' and
though she could not conceive of a pride
in 'such people' stubborn enough to hold
out against the high honours of an alliance
with the noble house of Limborne, yet time
was the main object now, and time she
could gain by a determined course of
obstruction. Some show of resistance, no
doubt, these common people would think
it needful to make before they snatched at
their prize, and in the meanwhile . . . .
well! in the meanwhile many things
'might happen;' and so it came to pass
that Lady Limborne retired to rest in a
more amiable frame of mind, if not towards
the offending Nellie, yet towards that other
offending person, her son, and the world in
general.

CHAPTER XII.

MR. ARMER FINDS OUT SOMETHING.

MR. ARMER had no difficulty in letting Coombridge. A retired Indian official of high degree in the Civil Service saw and was charmed with the place, and quickly agreed to the squire's terms. Rumours of the squire's intention to let Coombridge had filtered from the dining-room, through the kitchen, to the village, and thence far and wide over the surrounding district and great was the sorrow expressed at the prospect of losing such 'charming' neighbours. The village folk, however, were able to see some seeds of consolation, in the thoughts of the Indian potentate who was to take the Armers' place, and who would

be certain, as they imagined, to disburse
his cash in orthodox Oriental profusion.

Mr. Lamacraft was able to give some
information to his customers at *the* shop,
and there was in consequence quite a
'revival of trade.' Most of the farmers'
and labourers' wives discovered they were
in immediate pressing want of a yard or
two of calico, some trifle in the way of
needles or cotton, tea or sugar; for Mr.
Lamacraft's trade was of an all-embracing
nature, and though his high prices, and the
inferiority of his goods, drove most of the
farming folk to Exeter—not to speak of
the temptations of a jaunt into that ancient
city under the specious pretence of
'shopping'—yet the noble system of 'tick'
procured him a large, and alas! lasting
clientèle among the labourers, for they
owed 'at the shop,' and they had to go on
owing to keep Mr. Lamacraft in good
temper. On this occasion, however, he
'pardonably chuckled' at the rapid way

in which his goods disappeared as he narrated to each person his experience of the nabob.

'Not a bit like squire,' said he, 'a yaller-favoured kind of a man, a praper, tall gentleman, so thin's a needle; very 'igh manners he've a-got to un; spoke up so sharp, her did, anyone could see as he were a furriner in a manner of spaking, he come in 'ere, into this very 'denticle shop, stood just where yew be standing, Mrs. Tacker, if I may make so bold, he come in all of a hurry-like, and, says he, in a kind of commanding sort of voice, "Hi!" says he (for I was in the parlour, as you must know), "hi!" says he, "anyone here? I want a box of matches." And, as he was a-lighting of his cigar, I made so bold as to ask him if he was the new squire. He stared at me sort o' mazed-like. "Squire?" says he. "Oh! I suppose I am squire as well; I've taken the manor-house, if that's what you mean." And

with that he puffs out the smoke, and
away he goes.   I watches him as he jumps
into his trap (a hired one from Exeter, I
reckon), and a very active gentleman he is,
though his hair and moustarchers is as
white as a smock.   I do hear as he's
a mazing rich gentleman with a young
missus and a lot of little 'uns.   Well,
us'll be loathe to part wi' squire, and Mas'
Jack, and pretty Miss Nellie—the poor
folks'll miss *her*, for certain—but one down,
t'other come on, that's my ph'losophy.'

Thus did the flourish of the trumpets
and the herald's proclamation, 'Le roi est
mort, vive le roi!' find its echo in Coombridge, though, as old Lamacraft said, some
hearts were sad at the loss of the kindly,
if sometimes 'peppery' squire and his son
and daughter.

The new folk were to come into possession at Michaelmas, and the squire
snatched a few days from his work to take
Nellie for her farewell visits, and to take

himself to have a last 'go in' at 'the birds.' Poor Nellie was quite miserable at the thought of saying good-bye to the beloved home and her friends and *protégés;* but her father held out hopes that the exile would not be a very long one, for in a year or two he hoped to have gathered in enough harvest to allow him to give up his work 'for good,' and to go back again to the life he loved so well; and in a year or two what might not happen? Why, before that time Miss Nellie might be changed into my Lady Limborne, and all sorts of joys and blisses might be in store!

Two or three successful 'coups' had tinged Mr. Armer's prospects of a speedy fortune with the rosiest of colours, and had brought him to look upon this return to a somewhat distasteful life in London as upon a mere episode, unpleasant enough while it lasted, but soon to be over. Still both he and Nellie felt very melancholy at this leave-taking, and, as for Master Jack, *he* was plunged into the very depths of woe ; not only was he to lose all the delights of Coombridge—delights his soul loved, the horses, the fishing, the shooting, hunting, and the thousand and one pleasant fillings-up of time which these pursuits brought in their train—but the fiat had gone forth, and he was to give up the Bar, which honourable profession he had looked upon as an easy and, sooth to say, idle introduction to the life of a country squire and magistrate ; he was, moreover, not only to give up this cherished plan of his, but was to 'do something to earn his bread,' which 'something' resolved itself into nothing less than the taking up of a daily position perched upon an office-stool in the dingy precincts of the City; than which the sport-loving Jack could imagine no more hopeless purgatory.

So the squire had willed, and his son's foolish extravagance and consequent prevarication left him powerless to do anything more than to mumble out a few feeble remonstrances, to which his father paid no manner of attention. Nellie, however, came in for a full share of his woes, and greatly did he bemoan himself in her sympathising ears.

It was to a not particularly cheerful party, then, that Lord Limborne wended his way one sunny September afternoon about a fortnight after the unpleasant interview with his mother. Time had not softened that lady's heart towards her son's 'unhappy attachment,' as she called it; neither had the extreme difficulty with which she had avoided an open explanation with Lady Beldon tended to increase her affection (?) for her son's lady-love. Some skirmishings there had been, some rather plain hints thrown out, some delicate fencing between the two mothers, but no direct questions were asked, and therefore no direct answers were given.

Several near allies of both families had

been asked, before Lady Limborne had
been aware of the spoke in this matrimonial wheel, to assist at what she had
fondly hoped would have been a family
event; and, in the crowd, a *tête-à-tête* of any
length was easily to be avoided. Moreover, the Lady Emily was not one of those
damsels who are to be approached with
any very warm love-making, and she was
fairly satisfied with that amount of attention her hostess' son deemed it necessary
to bestow upon his mother's guest; and
so it happened that the Beldon incursion
passed off without any open manifestation
of any sort. The Beldons, not particularly
anxious for the match, were satisfied with
the fact that the young people had seen
each other, and had had opportunities
for the beginnings of intimacy. Lady
Limborne was thankful for small mercies,
and rejoiced to think that the visit had
passed off without any horrible *contretemps*,
while time was gained, and the game matri-

monial was still alive ; and as for his Lordship of Limborne, he breathed freely once
more as he lifted his hat to his departing
guests at the railway-station, and saw them
go away without any ' encursions and
alarums.'

Perhaps a man never feels so small as
at the time just before he declares his passion to the fair object of his adoration.
It is a great advantage, which *the* sex has
over us poor male humans. How very
plainly do we then see our various defects !
Covered over ordinarily with a more or
less strained forgetfulness, they force themselves into notice before this fatal plunge,
nay, they magnify themselves in a manner
most unpleasant. That which we are wont
to regard as a slight obliquity of vision,
rather piquant, in fact, becomes now very
real to us, under this strong light, as a
decided, and possibly offensive squint. A
large nose, we have been wont to observe
to ourselves, is a mark of a decided char-

acter. Napoleon had a largish nose, and there was no mistake about the size of the Duke of Wellington's proboscis. Many other famous persons were endowed with this feature to a large, not to say obtrusive, extent; but *now*, alas! as we regard our visage in the tell-tale glass, how obnoxious does this abominable nose of ours appear! Is there not, indeed, something of the *ridiculous* in its abnormal (for so it seems now) development? Heavens! *Could* any woman love a fellow with such a squint? with a nose like *that?* with such tusks, for example? so short! or so absurdly lanky! so pursily fat! or so waferishly thin! Few men, short of the Adonis, who airily throws the handkerchief where he will (*sometimes*, thank a merciful Providence! to have it 'returned with thanks'), few of us, ordinarily plain, average-looking men but have gone through some such humiliating self-questionings. Character, too, comes under the microscope at such a time: the hasty temper, the selfishness, the slight, occasional perversions of the truth, the 'oriental tintings,' so to speak, which adorn the conversation at truth's expense, a slight tendency to greediness common enough, a too great fondness for the 'cup which cheers and *does* inebriate,' a certain stupidity and want of humour of which we dimly suspect ourselves; all these, and many other unamiable traits loom up before us large and threatening. Can the all-important 'she' have remarked this, that, or the other? Is it possible for us to have concealed the flaw? Or *has* she seen it? And will refusal and the attendant bathos be our portion?

Such questionings as these make a man not a little nervous as he carefully shaves himself, parts and re-parts his hair, and endues himself in what he considers to be his most becoming garments before he sallies out to the pic-nic, ball, garden-party, or what not, where he is to meet

Araminta, and put an end to the tortures
of suspense, which are turning his being
topsy-turvy, and making a tantalus-woe of
his life. Yet there are alleviations and
encouragements, or he never could 'come
up to the scratch.'

Why did Araminta permit him to hold
her fair hand one moment longer than
courtesy demanded, as he said, 'good-bye,'
the night before last? Why did she thank
him so sweetly for that song he ventured
to send her? for the bouquet which arrived
anonymously at the paternal mansion?
Why did she look at him in that *peculiar*
way in the conservatory at the De Robin-
sons' dance? And so he goes on through
an interminable quantity of 'why's' until
enough courage is infused into him to bring
him to the last rush, or forlorn hope.

But there are no counterbalancing 'why's'
to comfort the poor soul as he 'unwilling
wends his way' to the dreaded interview
with 'papa,' which must needs follow the

s 2

rapturous hour in which he found he was
beloved.   How infinitesimally small do his
'means' appear, perhaps, to the rash aspirant !   He knows very well into what a
tiny drop of water the whole lump will melt
under the scrutiny of the 'father of she,'
and he would, though not a sporting man
or a glory-hunting soldier, rather face an
enraged specimen of 'big game,' or mount
the fiery breach, than hold that half-hour's
committee of ways and means with the
quiet and common-place-looking individual
who happens to be the author of Araminta's
being.

True it is that Lord Limborne had a
position to offer which few girls, or girls'
fathers, could afford to despise ; and it is
also true that, though poor for that position, his widow would not go unprovided
for: there are, however, other things besides
money which occasionally interfere with
the course of true love ; there is family .
pride, for example ; and with this on his

mother's side, and with the obstinacy and
ready pride of another sort on the squire's
part, had Lord Limborne to reckon as he
rode up the Coombridge drive to his interview with his Nellie's father.

Nellie greatly disliked, nay, positively
hated, all this concealment, and she had
many times regretted that she had allowed
herself to be persuaded into it on that memo-
rable Teignbridge day ; it should be made
as harmless as possible, there should be no
stolen interviews, no clandestine correspondence, and hence it was that she was
ignorant of much that had happened lately
at Limborne Castle ; she did not even know
that Lady Limborne had been told of the
engagement, nor did she know of the rage
of that noble dame thereat. She had heard,
however, from the gossip of the country-
side, and almost as soon as she arrived at
Coombridge, that the great family of Beldon had been staying at the Castle, and
she was not a little curious and excited as

to how that visitation had speeded. Every other feeling but those of keen joy and pride in her lover left her as she looked up from her book, and saw from the windows the gallant figure of Lord Limborne as he rode up to the house; nor did *he* fail to perceive his pretty *fiancée*, and to mark the ready blush and the more than pleased look which greeted him. Hudson showed him into the drawing-room and departed, as quickly as his dignity would permit him, to send after the squire, who was 'somewhere about the place,' and Nellie and Lord Limborne were alone together, after what had seemed to both of them an interminable space of time.

Such a meeting as this was may well deserve a chapter to itself.

CHAPTER XIII.

IT is easy to imagine that a few minutes were, shall we say ' wasted '? in the slightly inarticulate, and certainly short, sentences which accompanied an amount of ' konoodlement ' surely justifiable under the circumstances.

' James,' cried the sensible Nellie, coming to herself at the thought of all she had to hear, and probably to decide—' James, father will be here almost directly, I know he is not very far off, so do be sensible and tell me what has happened. Does Lady Limborne know ? I want to know about the Beldons. What does your mother say to it all ?'

Each one of these hurried questions came down like a douche of ice-cold water on the fervour of Lord Limborne, and it required all his art to conceal the difficulty he found in answering in such a manner as not to wound Nellie's sensibility, or arouse her fears for the future.

'I will answer your questions in their order, Nellie,' returned Lord Limborne: 'first, as to my mother; she *does* know. I almost wish now I had told her at first, but, as you know, I thought it better to break it gradually to her, since she seemed so determined about this abominable Beldon imbroglio. Faugh!' ejaculated Lord Limborne, with an expression of intense disgust upon his face. 'It is *too* bad of my mother to put me, to say nothing of Emily Beldon, in such an absurd position; it is more than absurd, it is painful, almost indecent. At any rate they are gone, and that, I am thankful to say, without any ridiculous fiasco; I shall take good care to prevent such humiliating possibilities for the future. As to my mother, as I told you, Nellie, she had set her heart upon the absurd Beldon farce, and of course she is disappointed. Now, Nellie darling, you must bear with her; she is the dearest mother in the world, she has starved and stinted for me, and it is to this affection of hers for me that we must trust to bring all things to a happy end.'

'But, James,' said Nellie, turning very red, and looking away from her lover, 'if Lady Limborne is proud, I am proud, too, and I will not, I *cannot*, however much I love you—and I think you know now that I do love you, James—I *could* not marry you against your mother's wish. Oh! I do hope and pray she will not be so hard! And, James, father *must* be told now, and he will be so pleased, I know, he always speaks so kindly of you; and he will write to Lady Limborne, and there will be

troubles upon troubles. I have thought of
nothing else since you . . . you spoke to
me, James; oh! why did you love me, and
make me to love you?' And the tears
welled up in the pretty eyes as all the dark
pictures of misery in the future, which had
been her sad companions almost from the
very hour of her betrothal, surged up before
her, and overwhelmed her. Lord Limborne soothed her as best he might; he
kissed the tears from her cheeks, and in a
moment or two the brief storm had passed
over, and Nellie was herself again.

'There is a bright side, Nellie dear,' said
the lover; 'why need you paint the picture
in such dark colours? I feel myself to be a
selfish brute when I think of you so wor-
ried and so unhappy, my poor darling. All
will be quite different from what your
fears would point to. Of course I shall
speak to your father at once; indeed, I
came here to-day intending to speak to
him; and when it is put formally to my

mother, and she sees I am in earnest, and
that my happiness is at stake, I know she
will give in; and when once she knows
you, Nellie, how can she help loving you?
We shall be the happier for these clouds,
when once they have all passed away. I
know it is hard for you, it makes my
heart bleed to think that I should cause
you any sorrow; but, Nellie, I will make up
for it in the future; when once you are
mine, no trouble or care shall ever come
near you.' Thus did the young man, after
the manner of his kind in such predicaments,
take upon himself the office of Providence,
and propose to shield his beloved from all
the rough attacks of outrageous fortune.

'You must not think me weak and foolish, James, because I have given way like
this,' said Nellie as she dried her eyes. 'I have
been so unhappy; it seems so wrong going
on just as if nothing had happened. I have
hated it so, and it has made me so miserable; but it will be all over now, won't it,

James? And almost anything is better than all this suspense. Do not look so unhappy, dear, you could not help it, you know, and I would bear a great deal more than this for you.'

Such a remark as this last one of Nellie's could only be answered in one way, and whilst that ' one way' was proceeding, the door opened, and admitted the burly form of Squire Armer, who was not a little astonished to come suddenly upon a very pretty picture indeed ; in which picture the sedate Lord Limborne and his daughter Nellie were the chief, or, in truth, the only figures.

' Why, Nellie !' he exclaimed, ' what on earth—Lord Limborne ! I *am* surprised—' but a smile on the squire's honest face showed that, if he was surprised, he was pleased too, as the guilty couple retired from close quarters with some precipitation, and Lord Limborne—for once in his life with a very red countenance, and considerably embarrassed—seized hold of Mr. Armer's hand, and **made some** incoherent remarks about ' dear Nellie,' and 'he hoped the squire would pardon——'

'**Pardon** what, my dear fellow ?' hastily interrupted Mr. Armer, pitying his friend's confusion, and **feeling not** a little confused himself. '**Here**, Nellie, don't run away, **my dear !**' and, as **that** young **lady** was quickly beating **a retreat**, the squire caught his daughter **in his arms, and** kissed **her** fondly. 'So, so,' he **cried**, ' *that* is **the way** the wind blows, **is it ?** You've stolen **a** march upon me, you little **monkey,** have you ?' But Nellie would not stay to hear any more, and as her father held her at arm's length, and looked at her quizzically, she struggled away from him, and fairly bolted out **of** the room, if **a** young **and** lovely female can be said **to do any-** thing **so unromantic** as to 'bolt.' ' Well, **my** lord,' said **the** squire, ' a pretty plot **has** been **going on under my very** nose, but I was not so blind as perhaps you imagined, and to tell you the truth, Limborne, there is no one to whom I would give my little Nell with a better heart. It is the fashion now-a-days for young folk to arrange these little affairs between themselves, so I suppose I must not " jaw " you, as Jack elegantly expresses it.'

'Indeed, Mr. Armer,' said Lord Limborne, ' I came here this afternoon to tell you about it all, and to ask your permission . . .'

'Permission!' interrupted the squire. 'Unless my eyes deceived me, you seem to have taken that for granted, young man ;' and Mr. Armer chuckled in a way which very plainly showed that there would not be much opposition on *his* part. 'But I can't talk to you here,' he went on ; ' come into my study, we shan't be interrupted there, and we can talk matters over comfortably.' And the squire led the way out of the drawing-room, across the hall, into the small apartment sacred to the gods of fishing, shooting, and the stable, and dignified by the name of study, though there was nothing savouring of the studious in the aspect of the room, adorned as it was with rods, guns, whip-racks, a favourite pair or two of 'tops,' and many other evidences of its owner's devotion to river, road, and field.

Seating himself comfortably in an easy-chair, and motioning to Lord Limborne to ensconce himself in another, he began :

'I confess, Limborne, I am not altogether astonished ; I had some idea that there were other attractions for you at Coombridge besides Jack and myself.'

' It is good of you to take it so kindly,' said Lord Limborne ; ' perhaps I ought to have said something to you before, but I did not intend to speak so soon . . .'

' My dear fellow,' interrupted the squire, ' do not make any excuses ; I was joking when I spoke just now. I am more than pleased ; I respect and like you, Limborne, and nothing has delighted me so much for years. Nellie is my only daughter, she is doubly dear to me, she is the very image of her dear mother, but I cannot hope to keep her with me always, and, if she makes half as kind and true a wife as her poor mother was, you will indeed be a happy man, Limborne.'

There are in most of us sacred memories, our own peculiar possessions—not often do they show themselves to others ; and the squire got up, and walked to the window for a moment or two, as this crisis in his daughter's life brought back painful, yet happy memories of the wife he had loved and lost long ago ; happy, for if his wife had been a loving and forbearing companion to him, he, on his part, had been a tender husband, and he had no evil conscience-pricks to make the memory of the past hideous to him.

'Well, well,' he said, coming back to his

chair with a suspicious look of moisture in his eyes, 'I am sure my poor Marion would have been proud and happy to think that her little daughter had won the affection of so true a gentleman as I know you to be, Lord Limborne. I must not let sad memories darken such a day as this——' After a pause, he went on, 'I don't know what the etiquette in these matters may be, but I suppose I must announce the auspicious event to Lady Limborne? Of course she knows?'

'Oh! yes, I have spoken to my mother about it,' replied Lord Limborne; and he felt anything but cheerful as he recalled the unpleasant interview.

Now Mr. Armer was certainly proud to think of the position his daughter would take as Lady Limborne, but he was far from regarding that position in the high and exalted light in which it was regarded by the dowager-to-be. The Armers came of a good old Yorkshire family, and had once owned large properties in that county, though the only relic of their once large possessions there was the advowson of the living of the parish where they had flourished, and gradually decayed. This living had been held by the squire's father, and when, greatly to the old rector's grief, his only child utterly refused to 'take orders,' for which career he felt himself to be entirely unsuited, he had, though much against the grain, allowed his son to take his own sensible course, and, instead of ekeing out small means in miserable attempts to follow some 'genteel' but choked profession, to take what money his father could scrape together, by the sale of the advowson among other things, and to go and woo fickle fortune as best he might, and with such success as we know of, in famous London town. Mr. Armer knew, too, as, indeed, all the world knew, that money was a not too plentiful commodity at Limborne Castle, and he did not

see any very great disparity between
Nellie Armer with good birth, particularly
good looks, and the prospect of a fair
fortune, and Lord Limborne with an
ancient title, and very little to keep it up
withal. Lady Limborne's remarks about
the Coombridge roturiers would have not
a little astonished the squire, who was
prepared for an effusive reception from
her ladyship, rather than for the haughty
rejection which her son more than half
feared on her part.

'Of course I know I must tell Lady
Limborne myself,' said the squire, 'the
question is—had I better call, or write?
It would be more courteous to call, I
think, but, though I have met her occasionally, oddly enough I hardly know your
mother to speak to ; and, therefore, I
think, perhaps, I had better write. However, I will do exactly what you think best
in the matter. What *do* you think about
it ?

Lord Limborne knew it was not so 'odd' as the squire imagined, this 'meeting occasionally and hardly knowing to speak to;' for his mother, he was well aware, would have studiously avoided any appearance of intimacy on the part of the Coombridge folk, even had they been disposed to make advances; and on the whole, and fearing Lady Limborne's already hot anger might boil over in scalding words should Mr. Armer seek an interview, he thought, of the two evils, an announcement by post would prove the lesser, for he could prepare his mother for the bombshell, and the explosion might thus be rendered less disastrous in its consequences.

'Perhaps,' he said, 'it *would* be better to write at first, and then you could *see* my mother afterwards.'

'Oh, very well!' said the squire, with a slight sigh of relief, for he did not relish an interview with Lady Limborne, whose cold manners and reputation for hauteur did

not promise him a particularly pleasant
quarter-of-an-hour.

And then followed a long discussion
about ways and means, not very interesting to anyone but the parties concerned.
The squire was disposed to be liberal,
Lord Limborne was the very reverse of
exacting, and he would have been perfectly
contented and more than satisfied with
things in general, and his prospects of
his dear Nellie in particular, if it had not
been for the grim spectre of his irate
maternal relative, and the dire consequences which would certainly ensue,
unless he should be able to curb her
resentment, and make her receive Nellie
with a decent acceptance of the inevitable.

The squire had not failed to make him
acquainted with his family circumstances,
his descent, and so forth; and Lord Limborne was pleased to find that his future
spouse was a 'lass with a long pedigree,'
not only because it was grateful to him to

think and know this of her, but also
because he hoped this would have some
weight with his mother, and considerably
alter her views of the 'roturiers.'

Altogether things had turned out to be
much better than he had dared to hope;
and as he mounted his horse, and turned
homeward, after a most delightful interview with the adored one, his feelings were
much more buoyant than they were when
he approached the hospitable mansion of
Squire Armer on that eventful afternoon.

CHAPTER XIV.

DOMESTIC DETECTIVES.

PEOPLE are often heard to wonder how such-and-such a piece of strictly private news becomes, in a way totally inexplicable to them, the property of a gossip-devouring public, and are astonished beyond measure, and sincerely grieved to boot, to find matters, which should be confined strictly to the bosoms of those intimately concerned, bruited about in a way which sometimes brings to pass disastrous consequences.

The 'little affair' which has been discussed with closed doors in ' my lady's chamber,' or in a solemn family conclave in the library, and which is, perhaps, of such a delicate

nature as to make it an impossibility for the
people interested to divulge it, is met with
out of doors in a most astounding and confusing way; the skeleton, which one painfully *expects* to start out occasionally from
the closet at home, breaks out of bounds,
and stalks abroad with an appalling
effrontery. ' How on earth could Emily's
unfortunate entanglement with that odious
and impertinent young Perkins—how
could that unpleasant story of Charles'
misfortune—have " got about " ? Whence
did that " family secret," so uncomfortably
hugged closely, escape, and fly about pro-
miscuously on the wings of rumour ?'

The reason is not far to seek. What is
the use of closed doors ? What is the
use of the most careful of precautions;
when there sits in judgment over every
family, a solemn court, a Vehmgericht,
presided over by the butler or the cook,
with coachman and groom, housemaid,
nurse, and scullion for its members ; which

holds nightly sittings in the kitchen or the servants' hall, where the affairs of 'the family' are discussed freely and openly; where each one contributes the results of his or her careful observations; where keyholes, door-chinks, the letter lying on the mantelpiece, or even in the closed drawer, are pressed into the detective service, and the whole 'arcana' and 'mysteria' of the household are subjected to a minute analysis, and commented upon with a dreadful freedom?

Very extensive are the ramifications of this 'secret society,' and, 'the awful way in which master goes on at missis,' the very 'langwidge' he used, the extravagance or flightiness which caused the 'langwidge' in question, the 'things which would have made master turn blue if he only knew,' all the ins-and-outs of domestic history are carried about from kitchen to kitchen, from servants' hall to servants' hall, by 'faithful' servitors whose only mental food is this gossip, and often slander, in which they take such a huge delight. From these lower regions the vulgar tittle-tattle floats upward; and not unfrequently in that peaceful moment when Parker is arraying her mistress for the evening, or is brushing her ambrosial locks before she retires to rest, some spicy story is listened to, which story is repeated with equal unction, if in choicer syllables, in the drawing-room, during that otherwise uninteresting period whilst the ladies are 'waiting for the men.' Mrs. de Ponsonby Brown would do well to remember, when she is detailing and amplifying with such gusto (strictly without disclosing the source of her information) some evil story of a friend (!) or neighbour, that that maid who supplies her with these interesting and exciting histories repays *her* informant with all the sweet fruits of her own peeping and prying. Good dames, who wile away many a weary hour in hearing and retailing such unholy stories, we would have you to remember the facts above spoken of, and to consider whether the game is really worth that unpleasant candle which you most assuredly have to pay for it.

Poor Nellie was the last woman in the world to tattle with her maid, and it was far from Lord Limborne's habits to gossip with his men ; hard it was, therefore, that these two innocent persons should have to pay the penalty of others' folly, and find, as find they did, that ' Lord Limborne's engagement with *that* Miss Armer ' was very rapidly becoming the talk of the country-side.

The events which rapidly followed Lord Limborne's interview with Mr. Armer soon placed our unoffending heroine in a very humiliating position, and added a bitter drop indeed to the cup of woe, which it was soon to be her lover's lot to drain.

' It's my belief as there's somethink hup,' remarked Hudson, the butler at Coombridge, who was of cockney origin, and had accompanied the Armers in their first great move from London to Devon. 'There's a somethink in the hair,' he remarked oracularly, as he sat down to recruit himself with an ample supper after the labours of the day.

'Lor! Mr. 'Udson,' said the cook, also of metropolitan importation. 'Wotever can it be? Master Jack ain't a-been and gone any more muckers, hev he? Though I'm sure it's no wonder, such a free-and-easy young gent as he is.'

'There, boys will be boys,' said the coachman, who had just 'looked in' from his abode in the stables to refresh himself with a bit of gossip and a cheerful glass; 'boys will be boys. Give him his head, I say; let him go free a bit, and he'll be all the better of it, after; he's a affable-speaking young chap, and he knows the p'ints of a 'orse as well as I do, pretty near. Lor' bless yer heart, squire's got plenty, for certain, he's too 'ard on the young 'un, never see 'im so down before.'

' Go on, Jim; go on, 'Liza,' said Hudson, with an oracular wag of his head, ' you was always a one for talking, Jim, and you think you can see into a milestone as far as anyone; but you're out of it this time, I tell yer. It wasn't to Master Jack as I was alludin' when I said, as I say again, as it's my opinion as there's somethink hup.'

' 'Ow you do tease anyone, 'Udson,' said the cook; ' anyone'd think you was a spink, or wotever you call it. Don't keep us in such a suspense, for 'Evin's sake.'

' *I* know what Mr. 'Udson is a-thinking of,' said a young housemaid, who, together with all the rest of the company round the supper-table, had been listening with all her ears to the utterances of her seniors. ' I know what it is; it's my belief there's something going on . . . .'

'Now, just you hold your tongue, Mary,'
interrupted Mrs. Eliza, 'there's no keeping
you young gals in your places: if Mr.
'Udson's got anythink to say, he'll say it
right enough without *your* help.'

'You always was a sensible woman, *for*
a woman, Eliza,' said Mr. Hudson, who had
his own opinion about 'the sect,' as he
called it, 'and you're right this time, *as*
usual; we'll 'ear wot Mary's got on her
mind when I've done, as is right and
proper. It's my opinion,' he went on,
with much solemnity, 'it's my opinion as
there's other changes, besides the move,
a-goin' on 'ere in this 'ouse, and I'll tell
you wot it is, that there Lord Limborne
has been and done it!'

'Didn't I say so all along?' asked the
cook, 'didn't I say wotever did he come
'ere to lunch and dinner, and dinner and
lunch, if it wasn't for Miss Nellie, bless her
'eart. Well, it's the best bit o' news I've heard
since my Aunt 'Ammond left me a 'underd

pound. 'Owever did you find it out, Mr.
'Udson?'

'Why, by the way I finds most things
out,' replied that astute individual; 'by
putting this and that together.'

'Oh! then you ain't *sure*,' said Eliza,
with much disappointment.

'Sure! I'm as sure as I've got this glass
o' beer in my 'ands, and am just a-going to
drink it,' said the butler, suiting the action
to the word, and pouring the ale down his
capacious gullet. 'Look 'ere, 'is lordship
rides up, looking kinder thoughtful-like;
I shows him inter the drawing-room; there's
Miss Nellie as large as life (which ain't
very large,' he adds, in a parenthesis); 'and
as I shuts the door, " James!" says she;
she wouldn't 'a called him James, if there
'adn't been somethink hup, eh? Proof No. 1.
Next, master and his lordship 'as a long
intervoo in the study, for I see them go in
and I see them come h'out. Proof No. 2.
Thirdly and to conclude, as the Reverend

Bolland says, squire, and Miss Nellie, and Master Jack is all on the "ky veeve," as the Frenchman says, at dinner; and lor' bless yer, *I* know, whenever I come into the dinin'-room they stops talking, and then goes on again sudden-like, like a 'ouse-a-fire. Putting all these yere argooments together, I ask you, Eliza, if I ain't right when I say there's somethink hup, and our Miss Nellie and his lordship's at the bottom of it, I arsk you?'

Mr. Hudson's 'argooments' were found to be conclusive, and all the ins-and-outs of the approaching alliance were exhaustively discussed in the council of the kitchen.

Now young Tucker, Mr. Armer's groom, who lived in the house, and had assisted with open ears at the conference reported above, had a chère amie in the Wreford ménage, and was, indeed, 'keeping company' with one of the lady's-maids in that house. The 'Mary' in question was of a

curious, not to say inquisitive, nature, and
Mr. Tucker felt that such a delicious bit
of gossip as this could not wait until
chance should give him the opportunity of
communicating it in person ; so, that very
evening, he took pen and paper, and with
squaring of elbows, and after duly licking
the pen to make the ink run, he indited
an epistle to his beloved, in which, after
beginning in the orthodox manner by
stating that ' this comes hoping to find
you well, my dear, as it leaves me at
present, thank God for it,' he imparted, in
somewhat involved phraseology, and with
some curious examples of phonetic spell-
ing, the fact that ' our Miss Nellie is
a-keepin' company along of his lordship,
Lord Limborne ;' and, feeling exhausted
after his unwonted exertions, he ended
rather abruptly with ' Yours affeck-
shnate, George,' with a double line of stars
underneath the signature, meant to
represent the kisses which he would

very willingly have delivered in person.

Theresa Denton happened to be one of those ladies who occasionally seek some escape from the dulness of things in general in listening to her maid's recital of the gossip of the lower regions; such a piece of news as this conveyed in Tucker's letter to his love could not but be received with eagerness, and, perhaps, rewarded with some articles of toilette of which the fair wearer at first hand might be tired. An excuse for an interview with her mistress was easily found in the serious questions involved in some costume alterations, and Theresa was soon made acquainted with the important news connected with the inhabitants of Coombridge. Some slight suspicions, roused in her maiden bosom at Teignbridge, had, in a measure, prepared her for this downfall of her own hopes, but none the less was she bitterly disappointed. Since the conversation with her mother, faithfully reported

in a former chapter, she had thought a
great deal about the subject of that conversation, and had come to the conclusion
that, as Mrs. Denton had said, there was
no reason why she, Theresa Denton, should
not manœuvre herself into a position
which should give her the right to sign
herself Theresa Limborne. That book,
which has been called the British Bible,
was well studied at Wreford, and, indeed,
so well studied in one particular by the
fair Theresa, that the volume, casually
taken up, would open of itself at that page
in Debrett which was devoted to the ancient glories of the barony of Limborne;
and though the story of this family was a
long one, and entered largely into the
history of the land, yet Theresa was not
to be abashed by any back thoughts as to
her lack of 'lang pedigree,' for she was not
by any means a 'penniless lass,' and if
she did not possess the 'acres of charms'
and 'weel-stocket farms' of Robbie Burns'

song, she at any rate answered to his description in *one* particular, and was 'a lass with a tocher;' and this tocher she conceived might well cover a multitude of sins of omission in regard to birth, and entirely overpower the odour of the grocer's shop, in a small chamber over which the fair damsel first saw light. The poverty of the Limborne family was very well known, and the wealth of Wreford was sufficiently well displayed in the gorgeous appointments of house, equipage, and retinue. A coronet, if only of a humble baron, was a bright and shining prize in Theresa's eyes, and she would gladly have gone to the hymeneal altar with a decrepit viscount, or a semi-idiotic earl, or one deformed even, if by so doing she could get the vulgar joy she had set her heart upon; but Lord Limborne was neither decrepit, idiotic, nor deformed, and was, indeed, an exceedingly clever man, well before the world, and if not absolutely handsome, yet certainly distinguished-looking.

Moreover, the consummation she so devoutly wished had not now seemed to be so utterly hopeless as it would have seemed even a month ago; for Miss Ingle's diplomacy had been crowned with signal success, and the Dentons already occupied that position in society 'to which,' as Mrs. Denton so frequently remarked, 'their wealth entitled them.' All the 'best people' had called after the Teignbridge début, the great Denton ball had been trumpeted forth to so large an extent that the dream of Mrs. Denton's life had been realized, and carriage after carriage had driven up to the gleaming portals, and there deposited persons of the very highest distinction, whilst an added lustre had been bestowed by the presence of the Limborne Castle party, including the great and potent family of Beldon; for, apart from the delicate manœuvres as to church restoration, this ball was a perfect god-send to

Lady Limborne, who found some difficulty in providing for the entertainment of the important personages then under her roof, and had seized upon Miss Ingle's hints at the gratification her presence at Wreford would afford, and graciously accepted an invitation which, at any rate, provided for *one* evening out of the dreadful six of the Beldon visitation.

'Two unmarried daughters, with fortunes of their own,' as Miss Ingle remarked in many places, 'and one unmarried son with such absolutely gigantic prospects of wealth,' were baits which had power enough to draw all the county folk, who were in the blessed position of that man 'whose quiver is full of them,' to the gates of Wreford ; and, because these ' some ' went, others followed suit, and at last everybody, who was anybody, called, and, after the due formalities, received Mrs. Denton's card of invitation to the ball, and 'had much pleasure in accepting the same ;' and so the seal was set upon the Dentons' patent of gentility, and Uncle Ben's fortune began to bud, and blossom, and to bear very choice fruit indeed.

Many invitations in return did the postman bring to Wreford, and often in the dances, dinner-parties, afternoons, and lunches (which latter dismal festivities do greatly prevail in these parts, to the waste of a day and the ruin of many digestions), to which these invitations formed, as it were, the keys, did Theresa meet with the innocent object, if not of her affections, at least, of her intentions; and there on these happy hunting-grounds, with all the art of which she was capable, assisted by a considerable stock of self-confidence, did she pursue the noble game in the chase matrimonial, and not without some measure of success; for she had so arranged matters, by a persistent placing of herself in his way, as to make it appear that Lord Limborne was not indifferent to her

company, and hints, and nods, and becks
were already beginning to convey an impression that the Limborne coffers would,
at no very distant date, be replenished by
some of the overflow from the Wreford
Pactolus. Now Lord Limborne was entirely ignorant of the above-mentioned
rumours. Miss Denton was very fair to
look upon, though too voluminous in her
charms to suit his fastidious taste; she
was an excellent dancer, she could talk
pleasantly enough, and with a certain
flavour of sarcasm, not refined, perhaps,
but enough to single her out from the
monotonous crowd of society damsels; and,
if he sometimes vaguely wondered why he
so often found himself beside Miss Denton,
she amused him, and he thought no more
about the matter.

Theresa, however, thought a great deal
about the matter, and was bitterly disappointed at the sudden downfall of her
house of cards, which the news conveyed

to her by her maid had brought about.
Nellie had been away for so long that the
slight suspicion she had felt in that direction had almost died away, and, in the
eagerness of the chase, she had forgotten
this pitfall in which now, alas for her! all
her hopes were to be engulfed. Some
very unpleasant quarters-of-an-hour, then,
did our fair Theresa pass, until the lunch
gong sounded, and she descended to the
dining-room, there to meet her family and
to tell the dreadful news.

CHAPTER XV.

UNCOMFORTABLE FOR NELLIE.

A GRIEF which is shared is felt to be much lighter; even as school-boys we liked to find others 'in the same row,' and as we have a melancholy feeling that our troubles are looked upon if not with satisfaction, as the French cynic said, yet with an unpleasing indifference by our friends, so it is as pleasing unction to the wounded soul to find others 'in the same box.' Some slight relief was afforded to the sore-stricken Theresa by the sight of her long and attenuated brother; and the desire which, at this sight, arose instantly in her mind, the desire to 'make some one else feel it,' was irresistible.

As soon then **as the** servants were gone **from the room, she began to open her** batteries upon this defenceless **citadel.**

'Good gracious, Henry,' she **began, for** in the absence of the servants at **this meal** of lunch she, together with the rest of the family, relapsed slightly **into the** former way of speaking, and felt **a** blissful relief in **so doing.** 'Good gracious, Henry, **what** makes **you** look so depressingly dismal?'

As is the habit **of this class of** æsthetic individuals, so fortunately **now** dying out under the killing **influence of a** well-deserved ridicule, **the** pensive **Henry had** cultivated a sorrowing **and** gloomy look, which was, as Theresa said, depressing, and, **as** she *felt*, irritating to the last degree.

'Well,' said **Mr.** Denton, before Henry had time **to** reply, **'as** Tresa says, whatever is the matter with you, Henry? you **look as if** you'd lost sixpence and found fourpence, as the saying is, and for the life of me I can't make it out. You ain't bilious, are you?'

'Father,' said the doleful young man, 'if the troubles of my soul display themselves upon my face, am I to blame?'

'Lor',' said his father, 'you talk like a play-actor. I remember a chap at the "Surrey" who went on in that way, and cut his throat to slow music and limelight in the last act, though I never could make out why.'

'Why can't you let your brother alone, Theresa,' said his mother, who always stood up for her son, 'you are for everlastingly teasing and worrying him. I am sure he does you no harm.'

'Oh, but, mother,' said Emily, 'it is really too bad the way Henry goes on. I declare, I quite agree with Theresa, I am sick of it; always sighing and groaning, and going about like a great wet-blanket.'

'Theresa and Emily,' said the irrepressible one, 'Heaven forbid that my grief should cast a shadow upon the brightness of your lives! I will leave you, therefore and go where I shall cease to trouble.'

'Yes, into that hermit's cell of yours, I suppose,' said Theresa, 'fitted up a trifle luxuriously for a pining anchorite—where you will mourn over your fate in a comfortable arm-chair, with Miss Braddon's last for consolation; but wait a minute, Henry, my dear, something is going to happen to the heroine; attune your afflicted soul to agonies of despair; prepare to tear your hair, and beat your breast, and all the rest of it; for Araminta is another's, or, to put it in plain English, Nellie Armer is engaged to Lord Limborne.'

All the time occupied by Theresa in this declamation, the unfortunate Henry was standing with the door-handle in his hand, ready to go off to what his sister called his 'cell,' while the rest of the family were listening with all their ears, and with open-eyed astonishment at Theresa's unwonted eloquence.

'It can't be true, Theresa! you do not really mean it?' asked Henry, anxiously, for once startled out of his affectation.

'It *is* true, and I *do* mean it,' replied his sister, with a spiteful delight in her brother's discomfiture.

'Well, I never!' exclaimed Mrs. Denton. 'Who'd a-thought it? only fancy! Miss Armer and Lord Limborne; well, I *am* surprised!'

'Of all the artful . . .' said Emily, and words failed her to express her feelings.

'Why, I thought as 'Enery was going on with her; whatever have you been a-teasing him about her for, then?' said Mr. Denton, 'and as to the young woman, why ever shouldn't his lordship marry her, if he wants to?—as nice a looking little gell as ever I set eyes on, and as good as she looks, I'll be bound.'

'Mr. Denton,' said his spouse, 'I'm as-

tonished at you;' and darting a look of
disgust at her husband, who was totally
ignorant of the *other* plans this engagement had upset, and was quite at a loss to
understand all this fuss and indignation,
Mrs. Denton hastened out of the room to
bestow what consolation she could. upon
her afflicted son, who had disappeared in
the general consternation at Theresa's
news.

It was unfortunate that Nellie and her
brother should have chosen that very afternoon to call at Wreford and pay a farewell
visit to the Dentons, in view of the approaching migration of the Coombridge
family to London.

'I hear a carriage,' said the languid
Emily, who was lounging in a comfortable
chair and beguiling the afternoon hours
with a novel. 'Do look out, Theresa, and
see who it is. I expect it is Charlotte
Ingle; she said she might come over this
afternoon.'

Theresa was sitting by the window, manufacturing some elegant trifle in crewels, feeling exceedingly dull, and quite ready for anything which should vary the monotony of the proceedings.

'Well, I declare!' she exclaimed, peering out so as to see and not be seen by the approaching visitors, 'if it isn't the Armers. Now we shall hear all about this engagement; it is abominable the way that girl has fished for him.'

' And caught him, too, my dear Theresa,' said Emily, spitefully, not unaware of her sister's designs in that quarter. ' What a rage Henry was in at lunch ; it was too bad of you to chaff him like that, Theresa.'

'Oh, I've no patience with his nonsense, making such an open idiot of himself about that little chit of a thing; moping and going about with such sentimental airs and graces. What on earth the men can see in her to make such fools of them-

selves I cannot see. A little mincing crea-
ture like that!'

Theresa was of a large order of architecture, and had a natural abhorrence, not
unattended with envy, for the 'petite' in
feminine loveliness.

Just then Mrs. Denton sailed into the
room in all the magnificence of her afternoon attire.

'I heard a carriage coming, girls,' she
said, with a questioning look.

'Yes, it's those horrid Armers,' said
Theresa, instantly changing her tone, however, and assuming her society gush as
the door opened and Nellie and Jack were
announced. '*So* glad to see you, Nellie,'
she exclaimed, running up to her and kissing her with effusion; 'we are all quite
woe-begone to think that you are going
away for good; it is *too* horrid of your
father; and what *will* a certain person
say?' she went on, archly, with a very keen
look at Nellie to see how the shot sped.

'You *must* allow me to congratulate you, Miss Armer,' said Mrs. Denton, advancing to the charge, with mingled feelings ; for, if she was delighted that all chance of her son's alliance with the Armers was put an end to by this engagement, she was, on the other hand, grievously disappointed in her hopes with regard to Theresa. 'I am sure we shall all be charmed,' she went on, 'to keep you amongst us after all.'

'He is so very delightful,' slowly ejaculated the languid one.

'So clever,' put in Theresa, with effusion.

'So distinguished!' added Mrs. Denton.

And three pairs of inquisitive eyes peered curiously at the unfortunate Nellie, who was confounded beyond measure to find her most sacred affairs the common property of the Dentons, and consequently of the world at large. Only one day had passed since her lover's interview with Mr. Armer, and it was only yesterday that Mr. Armer had despatched the important

missive announcing the event to Lady
Limborne.

'How *could* it have got about like this?'
Nellie asked herself, unconscious of the
detective powers of Hudson and Company.
Perfectly unprepared for such salvoes of
congratulation, confused beyond expression
at the suddenness and the unexpected
nature of these attacks, she blushed a deep
red, and turned helplessly to Jack for
assistance.

'Oh, ah,' stammered that young man,
himself considerably dumbfounded. 'Ah,
so kind of you, don't you know. I, ah, it
is—er—very good of you. I am sure my
sister is much obliged ;' and he gazed fixed-
ly into his hat, and stopped his wandering
utterances abruptly.

The few seconds her brother's stumbling
ejaculations afforded were enough to bring
Nellie some small measure of composure,
and to give her time to come rapidly to the
conclusion that it was best to accept the

inevitable, and take the congratulations as matters of course, since the whole affair must be disclosed shortly, and it was evident these people were well-informed, though how or where they gained their information she knew not.

' It *is* very kind of you, as Jack says,' she said, taking the seat which the gushing Theresa pushed vehemently towards her. ' But how *could* you have heard, for even my father did not know until the day before yesterday ?'

Now this was felt to be an awkward question, for it was impossible to speak of the origin of the information, and a general accession of tell-tale colour to the cheeks of the Dentons astonished Nellie, and would probably have provoked her to a polite insistance in her question, had not the door opened at that moment to admit the rotund figure of the master of the house. Now Nellie was a great favourite with old Mr. Denton ; she liked him a

great deal better than the other members
of his family, and had shown this liking in
the interest she took in his favourite hobby,
and the patience with which she listened to
his disquisitions on his orchids, and on the
obstinacy of the Scotch gardener who presided over what Mr. Denton called his
'eating-'ouses.

'I saw your trap, outside,' he said, going
up to Nellie, and shaking hands with her
'So you've been and stole a march on us
all, 'ave you? Well, well! boys will be boys,
and gells will be gells, and I wish you joy
with all my heart, though I *did* 'ope as it
might a-been other ways;' and he gave a
sly look at Nellie, but seeing she looked
flushed and uncomfortable, and knowing
from experience that she had probably
suffered something from the tongues of
Theresa and Emily, he earned her ever-
lasting gratitude by adding, 'Now, do
you come along of me, I've got some real
beauties out in the 'ouses, and it's a real

pleasure to me to get some one who appreciates 'em ;' and with that he bustled out of the room, opening the door for Nellie, and leaving her brother to the tender mercies of his interesting family. Poor Jack was no match for the Court of Inquisition which now sat upon him, and the severe cross-examination to which he was subjected drew from him all that he knew of the 'when,' 'where,' and 'how,' of his sister's love-affairs, and reduced him to a state of mental chaos from which he did not emerge until he and his sister were well on their way home.

It was felt by the Dentons that it would be the very height of pure selfishness to keep such a spicy piece of news to themselves, and, as soon as they had exhausted their vocabulary of astonishment and spite, they ordered round the barouche and departed on a tour of visits ; and were, indeed, able to make some social capital out of Theresa's disappointment, for the importance of their news broke down the barriers of reserve in one or two 'county families' who were intending 'only just to *know* them, don't you know.'

Delighted, also, was the fair Theresa to pose as a 'blighted being,' and her airs and graces, half-sighs, and general conscious appearance, gave colour to the slight reports which had already got abroad, and caused the observant to remark that ' there had been something after all between Lord Limborne and that Denton girl.' To be 'talked of' in connection with a peer was pure joy to Theresa's vulgar soul, and she was, besides, quite shrewd enough to see that, if anything *should* occur to break off the alliance in question, the more her name was mixed up with his lordship's the better for her plans.

Largely did Nellie exercise her brains in puzzling over the problem as to how the Dentons could possibly have heard of events which she had fondly imagined were

known only to the parties intimately concerned, and severe was the 'wigging'
which descended upon the ingenuous Jack
when his sister compelled him to confess
the extent of his revelations.

' Why on earth did you leave me, then ?'
said he. 'What could a fellow do? They
were all down on me at once, and took the
words out of my mouth. There was the
fat one gushing, and the lean one wiring
at me, and the mother egging them both
on; it was awful! It was mean of you
to bolt, and leave me in the lurch.'

Thus did the young man turn the tables
on his sister, who, indeed, soon ceased to
talk, and occupied herself during the rest
of the drive in anxious thought as to how
this premature leaking out of her engagement would affect the two persons most concerned. If it could only have been kept
secret until some formal communication
had been made to Lady Limborne, and an
answer returned, even if that answer

should be, as Nellie feared it might be, an
unfavourable one, nobody but her own
people and Lord Limborne need know
anything about it, and she and her lover
could wait for better days ; but to appear
before the world as one whom Lord Limborne would marry, but whom Lady Limborne refused to receive as her son's wife !
The very thought made Nellie crimson.
How could she ever hold up her head
again in such a case? How *could* these
people have found it all out? What a
wretched position she would be placed in
if Lady Limborne were obdurate ! And
how dire would her father's rage be if his
daughter were slighted in this way ! Altogether poor Nellie had a very unpleasant
experience of the old proverb anent the
course of true love, and the occasional
want of smoothness in that course, as she
painfully considered all these matters.

CHAPTER XVI.

LADY LIMBORNE WILL NOT HEAR REASON.

THE polite letter-writer, all-embracing though its scope may be, contains no form suited to Mr. Armer's requirements as he sits down in his study to indite the important epistle to Lady Limborne anent her son's intentions towards *his* Nellie; and the squire found considerable difficulty in producing such a letter as entirely satisfied him; for, first of all, he knew but little of the person he was addressing, and was thus, at the very outset, labouring under a plain disadvantage. 'Tis true he had been introduced to her, and had even met her some two or three times, and this warranted him beginning

with a 'Dear Lady Limborne' instead of
the more formal 'My lady;' but, having
travelled thus far, with date and address
above, he was forced to pause and consider how to place things in a light which
should be agreeable to the party written
to ; and, as he sat back in his chair and
pondered over the matter, it dawned upon
him that her ladyship had not shown any
particular cordiality to him or his. True,
she had called, and the call, with its cere-
monious return, had been repeated at
lengthened intervals, but there had been no
approach to anything like cordiality on her
part, and, in truth, her attitude had been
rather repellent than otherwise. As, then,
the squire began to inquire of his mind
and memory, he lost, in a measure, the
easy-going confidence in Lady Limborne's
delighted acquiescence in these matrimonial arrangements.

His ready pride rose up and impelled
him to write a somewhat curt statement of

facts, and he produced under these feelings
a letter which, on reading, appeared more
like the statements on the charge-sheets at
petty sessions than the announcement of
anything so soft and pleasing as the first
approaches to connubial bliss.

'Pshaw!' said he to himself, 'this won't
do at all, this "stand and deliver" style will
break off negotiations at once; and yet,
I can't Kootoo to my lady; they are as poor
as Job, and she ought to be delighted. I
must steer clear between the two extremes;'
and he viciously tore up his performance.

It was, however, by no means an easy
matter to get past the Scylla of *his* pride,
without falling into the Charybdis of *her*
pride, and quite a number of torn-up
epistles bore witness to the severity of his
exercisings before he succeeded in producing 'the very thing.' He spoke of his
astonishment at the whole affair; he artfully
enlarged upon his esteem, and he might
say his affection, for Lord Limborne; he

praised him in no measured terms; he even alluded slightly and delicately to his appreciation of the honour to be derived by him and his daughter from such a connection, and mentioned the great pleasure it would give him to see his dear daughter united to one combining so many good qualities, &c., &c.; he remarked that he was glad to be in a position which enabled him to provide something towards the material comfort of the young couple; and he ended by trusting that Lady Limborne would be as pleased as he was, and by proposing to wait upon her, as soon as he received her reply, with a view to discussing those business matters which alas! enter even into the sacred rites of Cupid and Hymen.

Now Lady Limborne had obstinately refused to believe that her son would persevere against her expressed wish and will; she thought that, at any rate, it would be some time before Lord Limborne took any *decided* step in a matter about which she had declared her views so very strongly; she expected he would return to the subject again and again, and, in spite of her expressed desire that the affair should not be alluded to between them, she had prepared very cogent arguments, and had conceived of many excellent plans and 'ways of putting things,' and had at length persuaded herself that James would after all see things in a proper light and give way to her now, as, indeed, he always *had* given way, hitherto. She did not reckon, however, with the power of the little god with the bow and arrows, with the many fascinating qualities of the fair Helen, or with that very considerable proportion of obstinacy and pride which her son had received as a birth-gift from herself.

Having persuaded herself that James was giving way, chiefly because he had obeyed her and had not spoken to her on the tabooed subject, and secondly from some hints which had dropped from the

voluminous Miss **Ingle as to** the supposed
attentions of Lord Limborne to the vulgar
but golden Denton girl—attentions which
she determined to nip in the bud as soon
as this Armer entanglement (as she called
it) **should be** definitely finished with—hav-
ing come to these conclusions, she had
altered **her** tone, and had almost **gone**
back to **the old** affectionate intercourse
with her son, greatly to Lord Limborne's
delight, who, on *his* part, saw in these re-
newed amenities, and this pleasant return
to pleasant relations, a giving way **on his**
mother's side, and a sign that, after a show
of resistance, to avoid the appearance of
inconsistency, she would bow to the inevitable, and receive his beautiful Nellie
as her daughter-in-law to be ; once received,
even on the coldest of footings, his partial
thoughts could conceive of no one able **to
resist** such **a** battery **of** charms as was at
the disposal of **his** inamorita, and he was
indulging himself **in** pleasing visions of

domestic bliss with a lovely and amiable
wife, and a complacent mother, when he
found it necessary to prepare his mother
for the advent of that letter which caused
the squire such mental exercisings in the
writing.

It is always difficult to open again a
subject which has been tacitly tabooed,
and this difficulty is the greater when the
subject has been the cause of wars and
tumults ; and though there *are* some people
who delight in the 'give and take' of
wordy warfare, and live most easily and
comfortably (to themselves strictly) in an
atmosphere of domestic 'row,' most of
us, including, in this case, Lord Limborne, have a nervous horror of breaking
the peace, and will, indeed, go through a
certain amount of discomfort and restraint
rather than assist at the opening of old
wounds. It was, then, with considerable
hesitation that he approached Lady Limborne on the evening of his 'explanation'

with Mr. Armer, with the necessity of informing her of what he had been doing and what was yet to be done.

'I have been over to Coombridge this afternoon, mother,' he said, after dinner, when the servants had left them to their dessert; making a bold plunge into the midst of things at once.

This announcement was sufficiently annoying and even alarming to Lady Limborne, and roused her somewhat from her fancied security in her son's obedience to her wishes.

' I thought,' she said, ' those people were in London ; some one—who was it ?—told me he had gone back to his business, whatever that is. Of course you can go where you please; but I thought we had agreed not to speak of that affair again ;' and Lady Limborne looked at her son in mingled anger and alarm.

' I only knew they had come back yesterday, and I went over at once.'

'James,' interrupted his mother, 'do not, I beg of you, force on me this distasteful subject; it can lead to no good ; these discussions weary me ;' and she rose to leave the room.

'Stay, mother,' exclaimed Lord Limborne, 'you *must* hear me. I have spoken to Mr. Armer, I have his permission to our engagement, and he will write to you about it; you will get his letter to-morrow, and I do earnestly entreat you to be the kind and loving mother to me that you always have been ; do not answer hastily, think what it must mean to me.'

Lady Limborne was perfectly dumbfounded at this announcement, the house of cards she had been building these last few weeks was blown down in a moment ; and while her son was appealing to her she had time to see how she was driven into a corner, and must decide now, once for all, whether she would incur her son's anger and possible desertion, by refusing to acknowledge his engagement, **or swallow her pride and agree to take what** was to her the most distasteful action she had ever **been called** upon to take. **As all** these possibilities crowded into her mind, she saw she was entrapped, checkmated, and rage filled her as she saw (most erroneously) the craft **and** wiliness which had thus forced her hand.

'Nothing,' she exclaimed, in the heat of the moment, 'nothing shall induce **me** to go back from what I have said; you have behaved most deceitfully; it **cannot** be *you*, it must be those designing people ; they have entrapped **you,** and they want to force me to agree to this most painful mésalliance. It is a vile plot—how *can* you be so blind ?'

'It is perfectly absurd for you **to harp** upon that, mother,' he returned; '**such a** word as " plot " is ridiculous in regard to Nellie. I told you I had her consent, and what more natural than that I should seek her father's? I am quite determined in the matter, I have not swerved for one moment, and I must beg you to consider what it will mean if you still persist in your opposition. What is it you object to? They are of good birth, if that is your objection. I cannot see *why* you detest them so.'

'I do not believe in their birth, anyone can buy a pedigree and arms and so forth, now-a-days. Of course they pretend to birth; it is absurd; they are roturiers, City people, trades-folk, all that is most abominable to me. Had you spoken to me before you went to the father, I should have told you what answer I shall give, and you would have spared me a most distasteful task. Of course, you are of age, you can marry whom you will, a barmaid, or a dancer, if you choose; but I am certainly not bound to receive your wife, and I will have nothing to do with this most painful entanglement.' All the time this uncom-

fortable discussion was going on, Lady
Limborne was standing by the door,
where she was when her son's first words
arrested her, and as she ceased speaking
she turned the handle and went quickly to
her own room.

Lord Limborne's sleep that night was
not of the calmest or sweetest; in a matter
of such importance as the settlement in
life of his daughter, Mr. Armer would not
be likely to delay, and courtesy to Lady
Limborne would probably urge him to inform her of the facts at once; the very
next day Mr. Armer's letter might be expected, and the effects thereof upon his
mother, and her answer, filled him with
the most gloomy of forebodings. Of Nellie's stedfast affection he was well assured,
he had no manner of doubt about that; but
whether she would endure his mother's
refusal to receive her, or whether, even if
she did still abide by her engagement, Mr.
Armer would not insist upon an end to the

whole affair, were matters which afforded
him some very distasteful mental food. Of
Lady Limborne's firmness of character, as
she would have called it, or obstinacy, as
this trait of hers was called by others, he
had had ample experience; that she would
abide by her word was alas! only too
certain, and the equally certain results of
her action were almost too painful to be
thought about.

Of course, England is a free country,
and a man can marry whom he likes, provided the young lady is willing, and both
parties to the bargain are of 'full age';
but, on the other hand, great is Mrs. Grun-
dy, and she will (too often) prevail, and
come in, in a very obnoxious manner indeed,
between young couples and the satisfaction
of their loving hopes. The time for post-
ing off to Gretna Green and its accommo-
dating blacksmith, or for the scandalous
marriages of the Fleet, is past; and even if
he could persuade Nellie to set the angry

parents at defiance, and marry him despite all this absurd opposition, the unpleas-antnesses of such a marriage were too evident, and the disagreeable consequences would still have to be faced.

The whole affair was simply maddening; here were two people attached to one another, position, means, *everything* satis-factory, the girl's parent most willing and even eager for the match, and foolish family pride, in the person of Lady Limborne, was to step in and very effectually to 'forbid the banns.' There did not appear to be any way out of the tangle, and Lord Lim-borne could only hope that the chapter of accidents might have some unexpected turn of the wheel in store for him and for Nellie. He was, however, not very hopeful, and events amply justified his despondency.

END OF THE FIRST VOLUME.

LONDON : PRINTED BY DUNCAN MACDONALD, BLENHEIM HOUSE.

www.ingramcontent.com/pod-product-compliance
Lightning Source LLC
Chambersburg PA
CBHW031341070726
47496CB00017B/1395